The Relentless Brit

Sarina Rose

Cover art by selfpubbookcovers.com/selestiele
Interior formatting by Author E.M.S.

Rostek Publishing, Melbourne, FL

ISBN-13: 978-1503081697
ISBN-10: 1503081699

Published in the United States of America

THE RELENTLESS SERIES

ACKNOWLEDGMENTS

Special thanks to my husband who puts up with my mess of books, papers, fabric, yarn and mail that litter every horizontal surface in our home.

Also thanks go to Space Coast Author of Romance and S.A.I.L of Melbourne, FL. Thanks to my wonderful editors: Deborah DeNicola, author of *The Future That Brought Her Here; Memoir of a Call to Awaken,* and Nikki Andrews, Grey Fox Editing. Thanks to Author E.M.S. for the interior layout of the print edition.

Sarina Rose
www.sarinaroseauthor.com
Facebook: Sarina Rose Author

The
Relentless
Brit

CHAPTER ONE

September 1941

I SAT IN THE ONLY diner in town waiting for my friend. Nothing special out the window or on the menu caught my eye. Its shiny metal sides, domed roof and big windows looked out onto the street and across to Hudson Park. The aroma of bacon, eggs and maple syrup filled the air. A glance at the stained peeling wallpaper and the cracked red leatherette booths baring their insides reminded me of my personal life, torn apart.

As I slid across the plastic seat to the jukebox at the end of the table, of all the damn luck, I tore my silk stockings. The jukebox cost only five cents a song. That was a plus. The silk stocking cost a lot more.

Oh, for goodness sakes, why did I pity myself so? Unlike many other women, at least I had unique job for a woman in the 1940's. I chased divorcees during the day while trying to convince my brother, the lawyer, to give me a criminal case or two.

"Come on, Mario, you know I can do the job as well as Miller. He's just a kid."

"Not a kid, a man and chasing criminals is a man's job."

If my present life bored me to no end, the past year had proved to be a personal nightmare. I may as well have signed my middle name as widow. Marie Widow Gentile. My husband had been killed a year before in basic training at Fort Dix and he still had a hold on my heart. Nevertheless I longed for something more, different and exciting.

I longed for the future. I sensed a change on its way. Either my best friend, Joann, or my only brother held the key. I realized at that moment something great waited around the corner. How far around the corner I couldn't even guess.

"Okay, okay, I'll be on time. Just breakfast, please," I'd said to Joann when she had begged me the night before on the phone to meet her here after her night shift at the Brooklyn Navy Yard. Would she tell me about her secret job designing war ships or submarines? Did she hold a secret American war plan or had she invented a new military weapon?

"Clerical," she said with finality. I knew better than to ask any more questions.

"Okay, for now. Just know that I think it's something more, far more important. A clerical job would not satisfy you. You're an engineer, for goodness sakes."

"Vera, can you heat this coffee, please?" I asked the waitress. Joann and I had gone to high school

with Vera so I'd known her for more than ten years.
We weren't exactly friends, more like
acquaintances. The diner brought us together.

Why did Joann want me here at this hour of the
morning anyway? Neither of us had to work today
and I wanted to get my housework done and work
on my book. Really early morning at the diner on a
work-free day did not suit me. On the contrary
Joann should go home to Ralph, her husband of
three years. I agreed to come because, after all, she
and I had gone through our childhood together. The
twine of a lifetime of girlhood secrets and happy
dreams bound us.

I watched a man I knew come into the diner for a
taste of breakfast. Poor soul. My heart ached for
him.

"Hi, Joe, what are you doing here on Saturday?"
He had been classified 4F by the military for one
reason or another like the butcher on the avenue
who had come home because of his flat feet. He and
Joe were the lucky ones if you asked me. Because
Uncle Sam said, "I want you," the other guys sailed
overseas to unknown ports. At least the butcher and
Joe wouldn't come home maimed or in a casket.

"Oh, just come in for some coffee on my way
home from the print shop in the city."

"So you're working again. Good for you."

"Yeah, you know, some guys there carry empty
brief cases to look like businessmen."

"Really? The Depression ended and now another
ugly war. What a crazy world God made! Don't you
think? What the heck was He thinking?" I asked Joe.
He just shrugged and left with his paper cup in hand.

I opened yesterday's Hudson Dispatch to the society pages to see who had gotten engaged or married the past week. Most of the local sweethearts I knew had already rushed to the altar before the guys left for boot camp. My name had been there once. My Uncle Tom had walked me down the aisle. I'd worn my mother's wedding gown, satin with a long train and big leg of mutton sleeves. My new husband, Gus Anatopolous, walked me back nearly two years ago.

Gus was the best. He'd enlisted soon after he learned that Hitler was marching toward Greece where his family still lived. Gus's early enlistment led to his death. Many more came after that, but we didn't know it then. Most men in town knew Gus, the young barber, and most mothers in town brought the little boys into the shop for their first haircuts. Gus would take before and after pictures, which he then proudly displayed on the wall around the big mirrors.

I dreamed about traveling the world once this damn war was over. Gus and I had saved some money for just that. I had enough maybe to go to Havana some day. Out of boredom and curiosity, I turned to the classified want ads next. Maybe a traveling job would once and for all push me to leave my brother's office. Oh, God. I should be grateful for what I had. I loved legal stuff especially the criminal cases for insurance companies. I dreamed I'd visit Scotland Yard one day. There'd be plenty of time after the war ended. I was only twenty-eight. I had a long life ahead of me.

When I looked up from the paper, I saw a blond,

blue-eyed fellow come through the door. About a head taller than me with a smile as cute as one of those toy bears named for President Teddy Roosevelt. The guy wore a shabby oversized raincoat. The coat did not hinder him from walking. It just blocked my view. Yes, Gus left me a widow but still female and human. I could still admire what was underneath the raincoat. He smiled at me and dropped onto the seat in my booth. Oh my, was he a freeloader?

"Hey, please, a minute! Who invited you?" I pointed to the counter. "There's plenty of room over there." I looked into those deep blue eyes. Could he be someone I was investigating for Mario? No, he wasn't. Something about his demeanor registered "interesting" to me. A thought about Gus registered "guilty". This guy unnerved me and the hot coffee in my cup spilled onto my hand.

"Here, let me." He grabbed a handful of paper napkins and wiped my hand and the table.

"Do I know you? Don't touch me," I said. Who was this stranger and what could he possibly want? I had to learn more. I was an investigator, wasn't I? Even though I still mourned Gus, I wouldn't mind time with another man. A movie? Dinner? That was harmless enough. Gus would understand, wouldn't he? Only God knew that answer. The attraction I felt for this man twisted like a snake around my feeling for Gus.

"Sorry I upset you. Before you shout for help, Joann sent me. My name is Charles Stanhope."

I didn't like pulling my hand away from his kind touch, but what would people say?

He took a cigarette from a gilded case. I took the one he offered me. He lit them both with his lighter and I watched him through the dreamy smoke. He seemed harmless enough. Besides, there were plenty of people inside the diner who would protect me if needed.

"Hmm…nice. What kind are these?" I asked and inhaled the sweet odor of tobacco.

"Turkish. Here, take this." He reached into his breast pocket and handed me another pack.

"My, thank you, Mr. Stanhope."

"I see she hasn't come in yet. She should be here any minute," he said, staring directly into my eyes as he leaned across the table. His thin angular features and a lazy smile closed in on me. I wanted to lean closer. His looks were enough to convince me to listen and see.

His eyes lined with dark lashes behind wire-rimmed glasses intrigued me. The blond stubble on his jawline ached for a touch. Who was this man? Where did he come from and why did he stun me so, intrigue me so, delight me so? I grew giddy and lightheaded just looking at him.

"How do you know Joann?" I whispered back, but he stood and hung his raincoat on the hook at the end of the booth. He sat opposite me and leaned across the table.

Me? I straightened up and sat back. My mind raced, trying to think about what his answer might be, but suspicious thoughts soon distracted me. I had never seen him around town. He was a liar who just wanted a cup of coffee? Then I saw how his shoulders filled out his suit jacket. Nice. His lean hands were what—? Nice. His strong his jaw was nice, too.

"I'm employed by the British government at the Brooklyn Navy Yard. That's how I know Joann. She suggested I meet with Marie Gentile. You are Marie Gentile, I presume."

Vera came to the table with a menu and he changed the subject. "Would you like something to eat? Toast, eggs?" Obviously he was stalling or making up a good story. I didn't answer.

"Marie?"

"No, no thanks." I couldn't eat. Butterfly wings filled my tummy. I don't know why I worried. Maybe anxious is a better word. I looked out the window and saw the wind blowing the leaves off the trees. A paper bag flew like a bird across the street. My heart was flying with it.

This charming fellow disarmed me little by little, but I didn't want him getting the idea that I was about to stay. Who knew his real identity and why I allowed myself this indulgence was beyond me. What nerve! He had just walked in and sat across from me and I let him. What a fool I was. I picked up my purse, getting ready to walk out the door.

"Please, Marie, just stay awhile. Joann will be here any minute on the next bus."

I stood anyway and walked toward the front door just before Joann stepped off the bus. I saw her cross the street, so I waited at the door for her.

"Oh, good you're still here. I see Charles. Come on. Let's sit down and talk. Besides, I need some coffee."

I stared at her and shook my head. Nervous

perspiration dripped down between my breasts. My insides tipped this way and that. My pulse fluttered in my temples. I was not easily scared, but here I was afraid. Afraid of what?

"Come on. Don't worry. He's not going to hurt you."

"He is much too charming. Listen, I have to go." There it was. He was much too charming and I was afraid of being taken in.

"What are you talking about? Come with me. He's the reason, we're here."

Back at the table I began the interrogation right away. "All right, you two. What's going on?"

Joann spoke up. "I guess you two have met. Shall we get started, Charles? Have you explained anything, yet?"

"Charles, please call me Charles." Stanhope spoke again, "No, I haven't explained, but I shall." His gaze went from me to Joann and back to me again. Oh, my goodness. Those eyes.

"I need someone in this part of the United States who is good with languages, fluent in English, French and Italian. We need a translator and typist to get leaflets ready to be air-dropped in Europe. Propaganda leaflets. Everything has to be done here close to New York City so we can ship them out without too much trouble. No way to get it done in England. The country is in wretched condition right now and crowded with German sympathizers. I understand you have the language abilities, the typing skills and the desire for change. If you want a change, Marie, this could be it."

"How do I know you are who you say you are?

You'll have to prove it to me before you go any further." Being a suspicious woman, as motivating as Stanhope would be in my life, I still did not know much about this stranger, a handsome stranger. I resolved not to allow him to pull the wool over my eyes.

"Suppose he's just trying to pick up some deluded young woman, so he would have a nice warm bed for the night," I whispered to Joann choking on words contrary to what I thought

"Marie, stop it. He has his own bed He never mentions women at all. Nor does he talk about any men friends. He is totally committed to ending Hitler's stranglehold on Europe and not get a hand on Britain," she whispered back.

I noticed his hand reach into his inside jacket pocket. Thin with long fingers like a pianist. Wait a minute, why was I mooning over this guy? Hmm, I might have to change my middle name from widow to the deluded one.

He took a small folder from his breast pocket and showed me his credentials: some sort of ID along with a British passport. He glanced around the diner. Joann looked over his shoulder from her seat next to me and shook her head.

I stared at her and mouthed, "What?" What's going on?"

"Marie, listen. Charles works with me at the Navy Yard. Don't let his American accent deceive you. He is a very good actor. Actually, he's an Englishman. His credentials are legitimate."

"I might now believe you, Charles Stanhope. Humph." I squinted at the two of them, "And you,"

I spoke to Joann, "why didn't you warn me? He crept up on me out of nowhere." I looked at her with a little smile. She knew what I thought. "What does this have to do with me, a boring legal secretary?"

I waved to Vera. We ordered coffee and donuts. In the few minutes it took for the food to arrive Joann and Charles set out to tell me more about the project.

"Just typing what you tell me, first in French, then in Italian?" I asked.

"Yes, just typing."

He tempted me. It didn't sound dangerous. Wait. I wasn't thinking clearly. Working with him was dangerous. For me, anyway. Why did his too handsome appearance, his too sweet demeanor and his too adorable smile enchanted me. I'd seen handsome men before this one.

A lock of blond hair long enough to fall over his forehead kept his hand busy pushing it up and away from his eyes. His speech fell into his native accent and I had to listen carefully to catch every word.

"You will have to keep working with your brother to make a living and to divert suspicion. My offer does not include compensation of any kind except knowing you will take part here on the home front to help the war effort."

Every word he said made me flinch. My hands were shaking. I didn't dare pick up my coffee cup. My blood boiled. "Hmmm. What war? Your war? There is no war here. Why me? For goodness sakes, Mr. Stanhope, I'm a nobody, a widow, a legal investigator of divorce cases. Anyway I already did my share for your damn war. I lost my husband, don't you understand? Your war made me a widow and I am not over it yet. I am not over losing him and you want me to work nights besides days and lose more of my life. You have to be kidding, of course."

"No, I am far from kidding. Ah, I see, you think this is my war, Marie. But it is your war as well as mine, isn't it? Hitler will not stop in Europe. He already has plans for the United States. U-boats are being spotted off your coast from New York to Florida right now as we speak."

"Not only did I lose my husband, I lost my dreams, my future. I'm done. Mr. Stanhope, doesn't your office, have translators? You work for a government for God's sake. You live in Brooklyn. There are thousands of Italians living there and in Manhattan. Again, why me?"

"Well, I have been directed to you by retired U.S. General Donovan."

"Donovan? Why do I know that name?"

"He is a friend of your brother's. He has set up an office for secret services at Rockefeller Center."

"Mario? What does he have to do with this?" I should have known my brother had something to do with this.

"Listen, love, just listen. You will learn how all of this fits together in due time," Charles said reassuring me.

"I don't think I will do it. But, then again, I do speak and write Italian, French and Spanish and can type well. Will you create and I would just translate? I've never done that sort of thing before."

"I shall be here the next month working with you," Charles said. "We have a war plan and we will be assisting the troops on the southern front in Africa and Italy. It is imperative the resistance fighters take back their countries. Hitler and Mussolini are crazed. They are addicted to blood and power and will not stop on their own. They are driven to lunacy and are of one mind, along with Hirohito in the East."

"Oh," was all I could muster. I thought he was cute, adorable and probably untrustworthy. For sure that was not what Joann thought. She'd been married three years to Ralph. They were in love. Mr. Stanhope did not beguile her the way he did me. She didn't stare into his eyes every time he opened his mouth or hang onto his every word.

"Today is Saturday. I don't have to work. How about we give it a try today?" I said hinting that I would accept the work.

"Not today," Joann said. "You'll start Monday in my basement." She handed me the basement door key. "I'm going home to bed with my husband. Oh, just be careful when you open the door on Monday. Don't let Sammy run out. He knows you. I don't think he'll bark. If he does you know where the biscuits are…on the shelf above the furnace."

"What about your parents…and Ralph? What will they think of me alone with a strange man in the basement?" I whined like a toddler not wanting to go to bed.

"I'll tell them you're working for the American Legion or something. Don't worry about them."

"What about me? I don't want to be alone with a

stranger in your basement either. Has anyone thought about me? What will Father Ignacio think if he found out? Of all people I would not want him to think poorly of me after all this years."

"How would Father Ignacio know? Don't be silly. Just do the job. Okay?"

"Maybe." I looked across the table at Charles and he winked at me.

"That should do it for now. Right, Charles?" Joann asked, putting her napkin on the table

"No, not quite. One more item. First, thank you, Marie, for doing this part of the assignment."

I took a deep breath and let it out slowly before I said, "Wait a minute. I haven't agreed to anything. You're asking too much of me of me." I put my elbows on the table, put my head in my hands, groaned, and rubbed my temples. My head hurt. I lifted my chin and squinted at Stanhope.

Charles continued, "Sorry, I understand perfectly. I have been too blunt. You are perfect for this job that may lead to something even more important. At some point you may be asked to go overseas."

"Overseas? You're joking, of course." I looked at his face for the telling sign of a joke to no avail.

Joann, put her hand on my arm. "Yes, we think you will go to Italy," she said. She must be involved more than she let on.

"I don't think so. I mean I love Italy and I would love to go, but some other time, thank you. Italy now is not like working in your basement. No, no and no. No thank you. Not me. There are lots of people in this neighborhood who can translate and would be willing to go wring the neck of a fascist or two."

You're the perfect one, Marie. You speak the language, know the customs, your English is perfect now and I will bet a shilling you can speak English with an Italian or French accent if you wanted."

"Fascists and Nazis are crawling all over Europe and you want me to go there? You two are really nuts." I crossed my arms, slipped down in my seat and looked out the window.

"Listen for another minute, love, this is highly classified." His voice was hushed. "We need intelligent, competent and fearless agents overseas. Right, maybe you are not the person. We shall talk some more next week. In any event I'll call you later at home and meet you on Monday; we shall not work today. Monday," Charles said.

"Yes, okay. Monday, I'll translate and type, but I will not travel overseas and that is final."

Joann said, "I have to go. My mother is waiting for me to bring some groceries." I tightened my lips and squinted, giving her a mean look. She needed to stay right there next to me. I would not let her off easily. I held onto the sleeve of her jacket. I needed more information.

"By the way, Charles, I guess you'll be staying next door at the wonderful famous Fairview Hotel?" I tried lightening the conversation. I had to find out his whereabouts for the next two nights. I hoped he would be nearby so we could meet again. I looked at Mr. Stanhope and found him staring at me. I caught those blue eyes moving from my lips to my neck and back again.

"No, I shan't be staying there. Actually Joann has offered me a room in her house, but I will definitely go back to Brooklyn. I have an apartment there and everything I need. I will contact you before I see you Monday. Have a lovely day, ladies. Cheerio."

He stood, taking his raincoat and the bill with him to the cashier. I glanced over my shoulder and watched him leave. I sighed, wondering whether he might be hiding something in that raincoat. Maybe a gun? Or maybe a wedding ring?

I tugged Joann's arm when she stood. "Oh no you don't! Stay right where you are. Sit. You have more explaining to do. What were you thinking offering me to go to Italy and what about a room in your house? How would you and Ralph have any privacy? You hardly have any now living with your parents and your pregnant sister. Brooklyn and Fairview. Your commuting back and forth is making you crazy. Look what you just got me into."

"You're right. Of course you're right. Maybe I am crazy getting you involved in the war. I am totally involved with this project. I mean, I imagine I am a little too involved. I have been missing Ralph a lot lately. I work nights. He works days. We live where we do. Maybe, as soon as Charles finishes his work there, I'll change to a day shift."

"Really, he could stay in my apartment. It is a really big place. Too big for me. We could work from there and I wouldn't have to be going home late. I have a spare room with a very comfortable bed. We'll get more done that way." I tried unsuccessfully to convince her. Who would want to work in a musty old basement?

"We'll see how the situation evolves, Marie.

Let's leave it the way it is for now. It really is not
my decision. We don't want to attract any attention.
Don't you think everyone in the neighborhood will
suspect a strange man living in your apartment?"
She defended her position.

"Of course, you're right this time, but then again
lots of folks are renting out extra rooms to make
some money." I waved my white paper napkin in
surrender and we laughed.

Of all the dumb luck. I had to work nights with
the handsomest guy in town and he bunked in
Brooklyn. Thinking turned to sadness. Sadness
crept into guilt. Guilt veered into anger. How dare
this uninvited man step into my life? Didn't he
know I still mourned for my dead husband because
of his own damn war? How dare he even suggest I
travel into his war zone? Chaos and anxiety rained
down on me like a thunderstorm. My head began to
ache. I said a prayer and asked God for help in this
tiresome time.

Then again, Stanhope offered an interesting and
worthy project. At the very least I'd have a friend, a
pen pal? Going to Italy? Maybe the big fighting
would be over by the time I came to that decision.
Maybe, just maybe, Mr. Stanhope would learn to
see me as a woman and not just a pawn in his war. I
would talk to Joann in a week or two. Right then
guilt for abandoning my dead husband's memory
snaked around my throat and squeezed. I squeezed
my eyes shut and swallowed a big knot in my
throat. It didn't go down.

CHAPTER TWO

MARIE AND I WORKED TOGETHER in Joann's basement office with the Smith-Corona typewriter keeping us company every evening for several weeks. The basement had walls of ancient rock, probably from debris left by the glacier a million years ago. Marie had told me that the front flowing edge of the mighty ice stopped here, and as it melted over eons, it abandoned its rubble over northern New Jersey. The coal furnace warmed the chill from the basement, making it dry and cozy.

I often brought big potatoes from the market with me and we baked them in the furnace on the hot coals. We found a pot on the shelf above the sink and we warmed canned soup in it on top of furnace. Marie had brought a coffee pot in which we boiled water for tea. Some nights Sammy kept us company, sniffing around our feet and begging for biscuits, but most nights we were alone.

A big old dining room table served as our desk. Drafts of propaganda littered the top before we finished each leaflet. The white curtains with ripe red cherries covered the ground level windows. Marie often sat in an overstuffed wingback chair, looking small and vulnerable while she translated war propaganda that I dictated. I wanted to crouch at her feet and lean on her knee with my pen and paper. I wanted to be close enough to Marie to feel her breath rise and fall. She had set off a desire in me that would never end. She was beautiful beyond any movie star or pin-up girl. Greta Garbo or Betty Hutton did not compare. I longed for her to give me a sign she might like me, a man with feelings and desires for her. I made sure to see her every night and not miss any appointments.

She avoided revealing whether she noticed anything personal about me. After three weeks, I had heard not one personal comment. It was all business with Marie, and business with Marie went well, but the closest she ever came to me was her brilliant smile, which reached me whenever she caught my eyes on her. I often drew her portrait instead of the political cartoons I needed to do.

She asked me, "Well, Mr. Stanhope, satisfaction rules, you know. Our accomplishments have exceeded expectations, don't you agree?"

"Yes, you are right, our work satisfies me very much and, as you know, we have completed the assignment, but not our relationship. What do you think? Shall we see each other again?" I asked.

In answer, I saw her memorizing the cherries on the curtains. She was not open to me. This gorgeous, honest, wholesome woman was not open to spending time with me.

"What do you mean, Charles? We've done as well as I expected. General Donavan himself has approved both the English and Italian versions. Didn't you say he has someone translating the black propaganda into German? He especially liked the one about Hitler deserting Germany, soldiers starving in the fields and retreating towards their motherland. I would say those were jobs well done." She had diverted the conversation again with a satisfied, cocky smile and an arched eyebrow.

"Yes, love, but I think you and I have something to talk about, something personal, do you not agree?" I looked into her rich hazel eyes and then at the silent typewriter waiting for words. I stood over her at the table. I rubbed the back of my neck. "Our work together is done, as you know," I said, waiting for a word.

She remained speechless and, after a minute or two, laughed and brushed away my question with a wave of her hand. "I am very happy with our business relationship and I enjoyed every minute of it," she said.

"I, too. Now I do not want it to end. I mean our relationship."

"Well, you know I will be working at Mario's office forever. If you come back to the U.S., you will know exactly where to find me. You have my phone number and know where I live. You can use it as much as you like."

"Lovely." I just stood there. I stood at a point of no return. She opened her compact and painted her gorgeous lips and all I thought about was kissing them.

She broke the spell. "Come on. Let's go to Ziggy's for a drink to celebrate our achievements." She put on her jacket and headed for the door. "I'll ring the doorbell and ask Ralph if he wants to come."

"Please, not tonight, I would like to go alone this time. When we've been alone we only had time for work and no play. Let us have some play-time. We will make believe we are on our first date."

"A date, is that what you would like, Mr. Stanhope? A date?" Marie teased with a deadpan visage. That was good. She was flirting with me and driving me crazy.

I said, "Yes, you know what a date is, don't you? When two people who like each other spend time together outside of work and talk about personal things."

"A date? Hmm… No, I don't think so. Let's just say a drink, yes, a date, no. I'm not ready for dating. Too many memories left, sorry," she said with a little frown. "It isn't you. I like you an awful lot, maybe even too much. Okay, there I admitted it, but now is not the right time for me, I don't think. Gus still has a hold on me, and then there's the war. The war interrupts everything including dating."

"Only if you allow Gus and the war to interfere. It is your choice, Marie. We are not strangers. We know each other. It is possible we could be good friends, very good friends outside of work, I daresay." She opened her mouth to speak, but I interrupted her. "Maybe even intimate friends?"

Marie blushed a glorious pink while pausing for a long minute to look at the typewriter as if she hoped it would give her words. I did not speak, not wanting to interrupt her thoughts.

"Well," she began again with quickness to her voice, "It's the plight of the world. Memories of my husband, my job, the whole decade…and you. For goodness sakes, you live a precarious life on another continent. I imagine you are on the edge of being found out by the enemy…" She took a long deep drag on a cigarette and continued, "You are much too charming. I can't commit to a date, which may lead to more than just a date. To be honest I have thought about you in that light, but I would lose someone again. Gus's death has been overwhelming. What woman in her right mind would get involved with a man from across the ocean who is a spy and roams enemy territory?"

"Maybe you, Marie. You know, in England, many have a devil-may-care attitude. You just have to live for the moment. Do you believe some folks even dance in the bomb shelters in England?" I said with a wink and a smile. I grabbed hold of our coats. "A drink, it is."

"I guess I could lose again. You know, Charles, losing someone you love is sad."

I wanted to take her in my arms to tell her I would stay and she would never suffer a lonely night again. However, the war would, no doubt, interfere with our lives. I would have to leave her alone many nights, even weeks at a time. My work meeting with German sympathizers in England and traveling undercover to Germany would leave Marie alone.

I understood too well what she saying. I knew

what it meant to lose someone. But Marie, my lovely companion of the last few weeks had stolen my heart. I wanted to spend more time with her before I left the United States.

"Come, love. To Ziggy's. You and I shall go, and poor Ralph will stay with his in-laws tonight."

Ziggy's Tavern occupied a long narrow room with a bar twenty-five feet long on one wall, a shuffleboard machine on the opposite wall and a jukebox at the back. I steered Marie towards two stools near the back of the room. Ziggy's was just a bar. Ziggy's didn't offer real meals only pretzels. Sometimes on Sundays Ziggy's wife cooked a big pot of kielbasa and kraut. Ziggy and his wife had left Poland in 1937 before Stalin and Hitler invaded. He had been able to give me information about the occupation from letters his family sent. I trusted what he told me. In turn I sent this information back to England.

"Ziggy," I said as I nodded a greeting to him.

He nodded back. "Same as usual, Charlie? Right. Scotch and water neat, for you sir, Marie, what'll you have?" Ziggy asked as he wiped the bar dry.

"Gin and tonic, Zig" she said, searching for cigarettes in her purse, finally bringing out an empty pack. I offered her one of mine and had a chance to look into her eyes as I lit it. I wished my lips touched hers instead of the white roll of paper filled with tobacco.

"So, love, what do you most want to do?" I asked.

Ziggy laid our drinks on the round cardboard advertising coasters in front of us. Marie's was tall and frosty, mine short and warm.

"A toast to us," she said and looked at me through the blue smoke floating throughout the bar.

"To a fantastic translator" Then, I added, "To our time together."

"To an end to the war."

"To Britannia."

"To the United States of America" she said with a smile, revealing a positive note I had not heard before.

We clinked glasses. As the sweet sound reached me and the warm liquid touched my tongue, I thought, I may never do this again, I may never see her again, and I savored the moment. I watch the way Marie toyed with the glass before she drank. I did not hear what she said. My thoughts were elsewhere. What might it be like to sleep in a warm cozy bed with her? She would fit under my arm. She would wear a white silk nightgown with a lace insets on the short-capped sleeves. Next to the bed on a chair would be her silk Chinoiserie robe and on the floor, peeking out from under the bed, would be her feathery slippers. Oh, my God. I was such a fool. I pushed the image away, sure that would not happen.

What would she want with me? I lived on another continent across the pond, in England. I was a Brit leading a dangerous double life cozy with the most infamous enemy in the world. Yes, Marie Gentile Anatopolous would definitely be more comfortable with an American GI to replace Gus. This man would be tall, dark and handsome, an Italian, fitting into her family and she in his. They would have children and grandchildren who would eat at Mario's every Sunday after church.

"Charles, are you listening?" she asked. "You look so far away. Are you okay?"

"Yes, indeed, I am very fine, love. Would you dance with me? Come. What is your favorite song?" I took change out of my pocket and walked her to the lighted red and gold jukebox. She chose *Maria Elena,* an instrumental by Jimmy Dorsey. I pulled her as close as I dared and we danced in the space between the bar and the shuffleboard.

She looked up at me with a soft glow on her face. Did I have a chance to be the luckiest man in the world? I held Marie in my arms, igniting desires buried to fight this beastly war. I had promised myself no involvements. Chances of my demise in the covert agency were high. Where would that leave a lover? Marie was more right than she knew when she said I led a precarious life.

A moment after we returned to our seats, she looked at the big Four Roses clock over the bar and said she had to leave. I studied her lovely features as she gathered her purse and gloves. I wanted her to stay.

"I enjoyed this evening, Charles. Thank you."

"Yes and it is still nice. Why leave so early?"

"Sorry, I am a working girl, remember?"

"One more dance. Please."

I couldn't let her go without holding her once more. The war might lay claim to one of us, but still as I felt her close to me again, I imagined living my life with her beauty surrounding me. I imagined how she would taste under my lips, how soft her skin would feel under my hand and how fragrant her perfumed bed.

Of all the songs on the jukebox some guy chose one of the saddest, *I'll be Seeing You*. I took Marie's hand without asking and we danced a little more before I walked her to the door with my hand on the small of her back. Outside, the cool air brought me back to reality. My time with Marie shortened by the minute and I had to leave her to fight and win the damn war.

"Will you meet me for dinner Friday evening at that place down the street from Mario's office? I will not see you until then. It is the end of the week and you will not have to get up early on Saturday."

"Yes, maybe Joann and Ralph can join us. I know she'll be on the day shift by then."

Damn, why did she want someone else with us? Afraid of becoming too involved? "I know about the change, part of my job. Listen, my time is short. Our work together is done for now. I would like to see you again before I leave. Only you. No "double dates" as you call it. Promise?"

"Okay, then it's a date. Oops. There you go. I said it. I am ready for a date."

I squinted, letting her know I did not believe her, but she let it go. I walked her home and gave her a friendly goodnight kiss on the cheek. She returned it gently to my lips with a touch of heat. I imagined something longer with a bit more passion for the next time we met.

"The Horseshoe Bar and Grill then, this coming Friday, after work about six p.m., alone."

"Okay, okay. Alone," she whispered.

CHAPTER THREE

I OPENED THE DOOR TO the Horseshoe Bar and Grill. Only the tinkling of glassware sounded while the bartender set up the sparkling glasses. I'd arrived early enough to secure the best table far from the thirsty crowd that frequented the popular spot after work. Tables dressed with dark green cloths and white napkins filled the middle of dining room. Green tufted leather booths lined the walls. I choose the second booth from the window. The upper walls were painted a deep cherry red and the tin ceiling glittered. Muffled music from the bar reached the dining room along with the aroma of baked potatoes from the kitchen.

Without a doubt I anticipated a quiet evening with Marie. Until last Tuesday night I hadn't shown any feelings, but tonight I would again. I looked towards the door just as she entered. Her face glowed from inside out. Her cheeks flushed and her lips were apple blossom pink. Her charcoal outfit set off her eyes and shining, wavy hair. I rose as she came towards me.

"Ah, good evening, love. Happy to see you." I kissed her lightly on the cheek. "I must say you look crackin'."

"Crackin'? Must be a compliment," she said. Her eyes twinkled in the soft light.

"Yes. It means 'great, fabulous, lovely,' crackin'."

She tossed her hair back and laughed. "Thank you, Mr. Stanhope." Her lips curved upward and she arched one eyebrow.

"Marie, what? Here I thought this was a date and you, love, now look suspicious. You remember a date…where two people who like each other say nice things…and perhaps share some fun."

"Oh? A date? I'm sorry, you're right. No work, all play I'm a little sad over that, you know. So this is a date. I'm happy about that. I never thought I'd ever have another date. Watch me carefully though, I may run out the door. My heart is racing. Being with you like this is new for me. So let's talk business for a little while. What are you doing next and what will I do? More translations?"

"No. Tonight is purely social. A date. Now, if you do run, I will chase you. That would be very embarrassing. Someone might have me arrested. My cover would be blown. Don't run, no matter what. If you want to leave, just tell me. I will walk you to the door and if you want I will get you a cab. Now, what would you like to drink?"

She perused the drink menu. "I'll have a Sloe Gin Fizz. Hmmm. Yes, cool and sweet." Her lovely eyes shimmered. "Are you thinking what I'm thinking?" she asked at last.

I took my time wondering if she were thinking what I thought at that moment. Then, she arched her brows again and tilted her head a bit, teasing me again with her smile. "Ooooh, I don't think so," I answered. Would I, could I, tell her I often wondered what hidden treasure lay beneath her demure white blouse? No, not with a covered table between us. Maybe with a blanket in the park. Maybe a picnic by the river. No, I wanted her in my bed...her bed...any bed.

"I'm thinking about dinner," she said as she looked at the menu this time. "How about a luscious, juicy steak and a baked potato, maybe green beans. You know, my uncle always told me this place serves the best steaks."

We paused as the waiter delivered our drinks.

"Now," she said, "what were you thinking? That's something people ask on dates, isn't it?"

"Oh, I am thinking. I would like to take you home, but of course, I live in London just across the pond but located a little out of the way. It would take us weeks to arrive there."

"Yes, it is out of the question for tonight, but not forever."

My head spun. *Did I just hear her say not forever?*

"Oh, for goodness sakes, I shouldn't have said that." She looked into her drink stirring it with her straw.

"Why not?"

She took a long sip before she answered. "Well, I like you. It wouldn't be fair to lead you on. I think of him too often. He is always here." She pointed to her forehead. "I see him in my dreams and I see his ghost walking up the street. He's never far away."

"He will be soon, love. You know, time heals all wounds as they say. True?"

"Yes, I believe it. But the question is, how much time?"

"I know what you mean. I lost someone special a long time ago. I cannot say I was in love with her. *(But I could say that to you.)* She was a very good childhood friend. Our families were very close and we were destined to marry. She broke her back in a motor accident. She died from swelling in her brain a few days later. I was only fifteen. She was thirteen. Now she is safe in a little corner of my mind. I think of her only when I think about my childhood and the good old days."

"I am so sorry. You know, I barely know anything about you. I don't even know if you are married," Marie said.

The waiter brought our drinks.

"To life," she said holding her glass up to mine.

"To long life," I added. *With you.* I looked into her eyes again before I noticed the waiter standing still at our table with his pad in hand.

"Sir?" he said. "What may I bring for dinner?"

"Right. Marie?"

"I'll have a steak, medium rare, baked potato and green beans."

"The same for me."

The waiter left us alone.

"No I am not married to a woman. I am married to this dastardly war and its consequence if we don't win. It is never far from my thoughts. I often dream about it as you say you dream about Gus. The dream ends happily. We all live in the country where it's green and sunny. I garden and raise race horses."

"That's a lovely dream, Charles."

"The damn war determines our future, doesn't it? It's pushing some people into relationships and others away." I looked into her deep dark eyes for a sign of how she thought or felt.

"Sad. Don't you think?" was all she said. Neither of us spoke for a moment or two.

"I'm for taking it slow, but not so slow as to dash all hopes."

"Hope, well I have hope, but…I…uh…I…." She didn't finish her thought. The waiter brought our meal. "This looks delicious, doesn't it? Real butter. Yummy."

"Quite and I am famished." We ate without speaking for a while. Then I said, "I dream about the war being over and the world restored to the happy order of things. And you, do you not have happy dreams?"

"Yes, I do. I dream of traveling to Rome, of seeing the Forum and the Vatican museum. I dream of having a family and the money to spend on it. I'd take my children to every country in the world, even China and Japan."

We finished our meal together and I ordered coffee with dessert to forestall our parting.

"That is a precious dream. I will come find you. You will be over Gus and I will marry you and live here in the States. We will travel to England often and visit my family. We will go to Italy and other countries, even those in Africa. There we will go on safari."

"Oh, I would love to visit England and travel to all the castles of Henry VIII and the Tower of London where he kept Anne Boleyn. They are two of my favorite characters and his first wife, the princess from Spain," Marie said.

"Yes, that would be outstanding. We could sail up the Thames to the castles along the river or motor to the castles in all parts of England…even Scotland. Yes, that would be lovely. Then what?"

"Well, if I were to marry again, I would make sure to spend luscious nights together," she said, "having long late night dinners, drinks and a warm fireplace in the bedroom."

We drank our coffee savoring each sip. I did not want the evening to end. I saw a light at the end of my personal tunnel and her name was Marie.

"I hope I will have children someday. What about you?"

"Children. Yes, children. Right now, I have a sister and three brothers. None of us is married. So no nieces or nephews. We live together in a rather suitable townhouse in London. I have not heard that it has been bombed so I imagine it is still standing." I stared at my hands before speaking again. She touched my arm across the table sending heat to my core and making me lose my train of thought.

"This damn war again. We can't escape talking nor thinking about it, can we?" she said.

"Right, I cannot, but you may at times, here in America. It is all an ocean away. I don't think war will touch your shores, but I am not sure your

President can deny Britain's call for help much longer."

"I think you're right." Marie said as she withdrew her hand.

We caught a cab outside the restaurant and I accompanied her to her apartment.

"Thank you, Charles. Again I have had a wonderful evening with you."

"You are very welcome, love." I reached for her hand and she allowed me to hold it. I didn't have to say much more. I felt as if I had been reborn. The dull landscape of the war that draped my thoughts changed into a beautiful spring garden. I now had a life ahead of me, a future. I could have a wife and family someday. I trusted that would be with Marie.

At the curve along the boulevard Marie ask the driver to stop so we could take in the view of the Hudson River and the New York City skyline. I liked this as much as Marie did. We stood at the railing where Hamilton and Burr had dueled almost two centuries ago. The river and the sky were a beautiful sight. The skyline presented us an eerie stage set. The sun had set and the evening had turned dark. No moon showed that night. The water appeared heavy and reflected the lights along the highway on the opposite shore. Marie turned to me with tears in her eyes.

"Will you be leaving soon now since this part of your work is done?"

"Yes. Not sure of the date, but definitely by the end of the month. Will you miss me?" I drew her close and she shivered inside her coat.

"Of course I will miss you, Mr. Stanhope. What shall I do with my evenings?"

She wiped her tears with her glove too soon for me to kiss them away. My arms reached around her shoulders and she laid her head on my chest. She buried her face and I rested my chin on her head. I felt like a Rockefeller, one of the richest men in the known world. My feelings swirled around like a tropical storm about to become a hurricane. At all cost I had to avert destroying this moment by trying to force my way into Marie's heart. I savored what we already had. I feared she would run for cover if I did more than just kiss the top of her head. She lifted her chin with her eyes closed and I dared to kiss her soft delicious lips, then I closed my eyes, moving to her silken throat before she moved away. I took in her perfumed fragrance mixed with her natural sweetness.

"Hey, you two, ya know the meta's runnin' I don't mind, but you look like you might ferget me here, ya know," the cab driver called to us.

We both looked at him, then each other and laughed before climbing into the back seat. We sat close together the rest of the drive without saying so much as a single word. She stared out the window to the lights across the river. Now she seemed far away from me.

At the front door to the apartment house, she turned to me, put her hands on my chest and played with my tie. I reached around her shoulders and kissed her gently on the lips. She kissed me back with a bit of passion.

"Will I see you again before you leave the States, Mr. Stanhope?"

"Sunday for brunch with Joann at the diner? After that, I am afraid I shall be leaving for Washington D.C. and then back to England."

CHAPTER FOUR

THE FOLLOWING SUNDAY I DRESSED in my blue
wool tweed suit with the shawl collar. I loved
wearing this outfit with the broad shoulder pads and
peplum. Both helped accentuate my small waist.
My skirt fell just below my knee. The suit looked
great, just a tiny bit bigger than it used to be. I'd lost
weight since I'd buried Gus. When I looked in the
mirror attached to my secondhand bureau, I saw a
sad face with lovely blond hair curling around my
neck and a thick wave over my forehead and behind
my ear. I didn't recognize myself. A thin drawn
face and sad gray eyes looked back at me. I had
walked, talked, eaten, slept and worked, but had not
lived life very well.

I hadn't enjoyed waking up very much since I'd
lost Gus last year. Until I met Charles that is. But I
couldn't release Gus. A stray bullet had slit his
carotid artery. He'd bled out before help arrived.
The hard dirt of the weapons range at Fort Dix had
served as his death bed. They'd sent his body home

and I buried him in Fairview cemetery. He didn't have any family in the U.S. Everyone was still in Greece. I wrote a short letter to his mother, but never had gotten a response. I hoped someone there could read English or the Nazis hadn't confiscated it. They were already on the main island.

Every night I would toss and turn a few hours until I finally fell into a deep sleep around three in the morning. The alarm would shock me awake, but I never wanted to put my feet on the cold wood floor to start the day. I would first say a prayer for the repose of Gus's soul and then ask God to bless me so I could get through the day without tears. I trained myself to say, "Enough crying Marie, get a grip." Enough because nothing I said, thought, or did would bring him back. I needed to get on with life. But as the days wore on, I would see him down the street or at the counter in Woolworth's or I'd hear him in the shower as I unlocked the front door to the apartment. Of course, it really wasn't ever him...just hopeful illusions ignited by grief.

I looked in the mirror once more and popped on my cloche hat with the green feather on the side. It had been my aunt's. It cheered me up some to think about her and how she loved my brother and me. We'd moved in with our aunt and uncle after our parents died. We were very young, just two and four. Aunt Millie and Uncle Tom were our earthly parents. I loved them now as I always had. Her hat brought back good memories and chased bad ones. I had planned a surprise visit to her today after brunch with Charles and Joann. He would be leaving early and I would tell my Aunt how I felt about him.

What would I tell her? "Aunt Millie, I think I am falling for a secret double agent from the other side of the world?" and she would say, "That's-a no good, *bella*. You need soma one here." No, I wouldn't say anything about Charles or maybe I'd just leave out the part about the other side of the world. I would just say he was tall, blond, muscular, handsome and adorable. I think he likes me. Oh, 'likes me' sounds so high schools. I wanted to tell her more, but honestly, I didn't know what to say. I couldn't tell her he made me tingle or that his blue eyes melted my defenses or that I wouldn't mind him kissing me all over.

I pulled the heavy apartment door shut and went to meet Joann at Sunday mass. I actually still attended church, which came as a surprise because I wasn't sure whether or not I still believed in anything beyond the moment. However, every Sunday morning the old habit of going to morning mass would take over as if I were hypnotized. My faith became more and more elusive. I could not catch hold of its certainty anymore. Nothing was certain except the end of life. That thought could be either exciting or depressing. Which was it for me? I still had to figure that out.

After church Joann and I walked through the crowd that always stopped and chatted in the lobby. I greeted some old friends but didn't stop to talk. Joann did talk to an old friend for a minute and I met her outside on the sidewalk at the top of the steps.

"Do you think Father Ignacio could give a sermon any longer? Geez, he surely knows how to lift my spirit with his barrage of intellectual insight into the Gospels. Oh and now I am so enlightened…. Never mind. That was mean to say. God, I'm really sorry. He is doing his best I guess," I said to Joann as we walked further away from our church. It had been our church since baptism. We had made our First Communion, Confirmation and been married there.

"Yes, but why are you complaining now? He's always been wordy. I can't believe you of all people are saying that about him. I thought you liked Father Ignacio.

"Yeah, I do like him, God bless him," I said, "but he doesn't offer much hope for life on earth, does he? You're damned if you eat before communion or have meat on Fridays or skip confession. Even the souls in purgatory are better off than we are in this crazy world. They know they'll have it better later. What do we know?"

"Marie, stop, please, it's too beautiful a day to complain. The sun is shining, the air is clear. The clouds are white and fluffy. After we meet with Stanhope, let's walk around the lake in the park."

"Sorry, I'm going to see Aunt Millie this afternoon. Want to come?"

"No, not in the mood. Give her my love, Will you? I'll go see her soon, but not today. I need the fresh air after working in that dump every night and sleeping every day. The leaves are changing already," Joanne said and bent down to pick up a yellow oak leaf.

"Sure, I suppose," I stopped at the bottom of the church steps and searched my purse for a cigarette. "Holy cow, only two left. I hope the diner has some. Believe it or not these things sometimes give me some sort of control. I think."

"Do you want to take the bus to the diner or walk?" Joann asked me.

"Come on. Let's walk. It's not far." I pulled her along with my arm entwined in hers as sisters do. We had always been close. We'd grown up around the corner from each other and went through all our grades together from kindergarten to senior high. We'd become even closer since Uncle Tom and Gus had died. She stood by me through the funerals and aftermath. I loved Joann. She was the sister I never had.

We walked down the avenue to the diner for brunch with Charles. The after-church families—couples, parents, grandma and grandpa and, of course, the kids—crowded the diner. Happy chatter echoed on the walls and windows. No one was concerned with war.

Joann waited for a booth while I went across the street where the shoeshine and newsboys made a dime or two. I bought *The Sunday Daily News, The Mirror* and *The Hudson Dispatch*. "Here you go, Louie, thanks." I gave him money for all three papers. I would read them later tonight after my visit with Aunt Millie.

The crowd at the diner thinned out and Joann and

I settled into a booth. Sticky crumbs dotted the table so I waved to Vera to clean up. Nothing had changed here in fifteen years. Always busy on Sunday mornings. The smell of fried eggs, crispy bacon and maple syrup still permeated the air.

"Joann, Marie, coffee this morning?" Vera said with a smile and filled our cups.

"Definitely for me," I answered. "You, Joann?"

"Yes, coffee for me too. Nothing to eat yet. We're waiting for our friend."

"Sure, be right back with milk."

I started to open the paper, but Joann stopped me. She stared at me over the rim of her cup.

"What?" I folded the paper and put it next to me on the bench seat.

"I have something to tell you before Stanhope gets here."

"Okay, I'm listening," I said.

"I had something important confirmed on Friday."

"Stop. You're making me nervous. Were you fired? Was Ralph? Is your sister all right?"

"No, Ralph was not fired. Neither was I, but I will be leaving in a few months. Ralph and I will be moving soon. We need our own place with a room for the baby." She became tearful. "I'm pregnant."

"Oh, my God, Joann, that's wonderful. Congratulations." I moved to sit next to her and gave her the biggest hug I could muster. "Oh, I am so happy for you and now Ralph will not be drafted should we go to war. So tell me, when's baby Romano due?"

"We're pretty sure at the beginning of April."

"Oh, my God. Guess I'll start knitting again. Are you thinking of names yet?"

"Probably Ralph Joseph for a boy and Janet Marie for a girl. Her middle name will be after her godmother, you."

"Thank you. Thank you! What does Ralph think?" I asked as I looked for a cigarette.

"He's very, very happy. Tickled actually. He is already looking for a place for us."

"Ah, that's great. I am so happy for you, did I say that already? Have you told your mom and dad already?" I gave her another big squeeze and went back across the table from her.

"Of course. It is hard to keep a secret in that house," she said with a laugh. "Really, it's so crowded. You know, now that my sister's husband is back from wherever he was."

"Are you feeling okay? No morning sickness, woolies for ice cream and pickles?"

"Woolies?"

"Woolies are when you want a food so much, you itch inside."

"What do you call it if you work nights, sleep days, then wake up with dry heaves?" she said laughing again. "That's why I didn't know for sure and didn't say anything. What is keeping Charles anyway?"

"You're right. He should be here. It's not like him to be late or forget," I said as worry filled my nerve cells and twisted a knot around my heart.

"Well, it's almost 12:30. He should have been here an hour ago," she said.

I had no answer for her. We'd been talking so

much we'd forgotten the time. But now, for once, I had nothing to say. Sitting here with Joann, doing nothing but girl talk was so wonderful, I didn't want to stop. I didn't want to leave just yet—suppose he came and we were gone? Would he come looking for me?

"Let's wait a little longer," I said with a weak smile.

I finished reading all three papers including the funnies. Impatience hounded me like a wolf. "So where is he? More than a little late now, Joann."

"Something must have happened. This is not like him. He is always on time at work," Joann said slowly, quietly. "I'm worried."

"Darling, what is it you two do at the Navy Yard?" I asked. "Is it dangerous?"

"No, not really. We decode documents for the time being. It is easy for me. Remember how good I was at solving puzzles? And he is good at memorizing dates, places, and times and so on. Decoding uses all those skills," she said.

My anxiety showed through the thin façade. I tried to hide behind it when talking about Charles. I tried like hell to hide my fascination with him with questions about his authenticity. "What did you get me into? Who is Charles Stanhope really? I took your word, but whose word did you take?"

"I don't know. He just came one day and began working. He's reliable, sincere really, seems honest," she whispered as she leaned toward me and put her finger to her lips shaking her head not to answer and to be quiet.

"Decoding documents. How sure are you that he

is who he says he is? I thought you had only clerical security clearance. He told you about himself and you believed him?"

"Of course, I did. After all he had security clearance. Mr. Amory, my boss said only good things about Charles. Everybody at the Yard speaks highly of him. He has a higher level clearance than most of us. There is not one reason I could think of that would say otherwise. No one has said anything to rouse suspicion. No gossip. Nothing bad. Nothing great, either. Really nothing to worry about."

"Humph. I guess he is what he says. I have mixed feelings about him, you know. I don't trust him and I don't trust myself around him. He is sweet and adorable. I want to believe him." I looked at my watch. "Where is he? Damn it." I tapped the table with my polished fingernails. Why couldn't he be working for the British government? "Sure," I said, "and the thing is that I am beginning to like him more and more."

"Marie, where's Marie?" she said and pretended to look around the diner for me. "You don't sound like Marie. Really? More and more? Wonderful. Fantastic."

"Yes, and I want to trust him, but something is missing. I can't quite put my finger on it."

I stared out the window for the next few minutes and wondered about those blue eyes behind the wire-rimmed glasses. Aside from thoughts of war, some other sadness escaped from them. Maybe it was just a reflection of myself I saw in them. His eyes together with his loveable smile and kisses Friday night had captured me in a net of confusion.

After all the evenings we had spent together, the drinks at Ziggy's, the warm lusty feelings he aroused in me when we danced and when he kissed me, I still sensed he was hiding something...

As the clock hands moved to two-thirty, I grew more suspicious of Charles Stanhope's motives and concluded that I had swallowed a bunch of malarkey. I drummed my fingers on the table, drank tea, went to the ladies' room twice, drank more tea, and put on lipstick three times. I wanted to go home, but I didn't want to leave.

I suddenly imagined him buried in the grave with Gus. Oh, my God. I pressed my palms against my eyes pushing the image away.

Joann was upset, too. She had shredded three napkins into confetti. She was obviously as riled as I. "Should we go home?" I called Vera for the check.

"No. Come on. Let's go to Brooklyn."

"Brooklyn? Joann, it will take us over an hour to get there."

"I want to know more about him now, before you get in any deeper," Joann said.

"What do you mean?" I called after her as she headed out the door. *Who were we kidding? Charles Stanhope kissed me.*

"I'll tell you on the bus," she said.

I caught up with her at the bus stop. "Where are we going again?" I asked as I carefully climbed the three steps onto the bus. Vera's husband was the driver today.

"Hi, girls, goin' to the City for some fun, eh? No charge for you two. Go on. Have a seat."

"Where are we going? I have an idea it's not Radio City." I said.

"To his apartment, of course."

"His apartment? Why? What will you say if he is there?"

"Hi, I'll say hi, did you forget about us? What if something happened to him? What if a Nazi found him out, caught on to him? Oh my God! Hurry," Joann said. Her knees were jittery under her purse. So were mine. What were we getting into?

"Oh, my God, you forgot about Aunt Millie. Call her before we get on the subway," she said. Joann always looked out for me. She was really a great friend.

"No need. I didn't tell her I would visit today, thought I'd surprise her. Otherwise she would insist on cooking a big Italian dinner," I said.

"Suppose we were to find him? Suppose we were to find him with a bullet in his head with blood and brains all over his pillow? What the hell would we do?" Joann bit her lip and remained silent.

"Suppose we don't find him? What the hell will we do?" I asked.

"Well, if we don't find him, we'll go home. If we find him dead, we'll call your boss. Since Charles works with you, we'd call the military police or whoever needs to be first on the scene. I think, don't you?"

"Okay, we have a plan. Good. We needed a plan." I boosted my confidence.

Charles Stanhope lived near the Brooklyn Navy Yard. The yard looked like an old fort guarding the shores. The street entrance had two crenellated stone towers with round windows outlined in white cement. Eagles topped the two columns on either side of the front iron gate. The chimneys from over a hundred buildings inside the walls puffed smoke. The foundry at the yard worked day and night belching fumes out over Wallabout Bay. The thick stone walls around the perimeter added to the old fortress appearance. It gave me the creeps thinking about how old it was and the souls who had worked for over a hundred years building it. Were the dead ones still around haunting the turrets and old docks?

Joann and I walked down Sandy Street past one of the entrances. Stores selling everything from dry goods to meat to penny candy occupied the street level of most buildings with apartments on the upper floors. Awnings shaded the big plate glass windows displaying the store's products. Trees lined the sidewalk. Low wrought iron fences surrounded three foot radii of earth where the trees stood.

We found the right address after a short walk from the subway. We were able to get through the first door into the foyer.

"No elevator here, I bet. Damn," I whispered. My Sunday dress shoes were not cut for this kind of work.

"Just a quick climb to the third floor," Joann said and turned the handle on the next door. "Shoot, it's locked. We can't even get to the doorbells inside there."

"Let's think about this. Come on. See if we can get something to eat over there." I pointed to the Café France across the street. "We'll sit by the window and watch. Maybe he'll show up."

Café curtains, tablecloths, and pink flowered seat cushions warmed the tiny space of the café. Thank goodness, it wasn't crowded, so we sat at the window peeking through the parted curtains. A few men and women who probably worked the weekend shifts at the Yard chatted quietly over empty dishes.

"Ladies." The man behind the register brought us menus. He wore a big white apron around his waist with a towel tucked into the ties in front. He was quite small so the ties went around him several times. He had a funny thin mustache fitting my picture of a Frenchman, but he had a definite Brooklyn way of speaking.

"Thank you so much. What do you suggest?" Joann asked.

"Well, the Sunday special is beef stew. It is very good. My wife, herself, made it this morning with the finest meat and vegetables from the grocer down the street."

"Sounds good. I'll have a big glass of water too." I said. Joann ordered the same. I slipped my shoes off under the table.

"No wine?" the waiter said.

"No, not for me."

"Me neither."

We watched the apartment house and the patrons coming in and out of the café for about an hour while we ate. We did not spot anyone else going into number 155 Sandy Street. The sun was setting over Wallabout Bay by then, casting a beautiful red-orange glow on the water.

"Suppose he's hurt or sick in his apartment and here we sit?" I whispered to Joann.

"I'm thinking of a plan. Something will come to me soon. Maybe we should've had the wine. No, we need our wits about us."

"I know. Let's go down the alley next to the building to the back and see if we can get in or find someone." I offered that somewhat scary idea and spoiled our reverie of a beautiful bay sunset.

Joann snapped, "And suppose we do meet someone? Someone big, nasty, and dangerous? It is wartime. We're just two helpless, defenseless females. No, I can't. Let's go home. I have to think of the baby. Come on."

"Listen, girlfriend, we came this far. Don't back out on me now." I looked around the café. Other patrons had left and so we remained alone with our host. He paced behind the counter while talking on the old candlestick telephone behind the counter.

"Most people are probably home having Sunday night supper. That's good. Less people on the street to bother us and if someone does…" I whispered and opened my purse wide and enough for Joann to look inside.

"Look at this pretty face powder compact I bought yesterday, Joann. Don't you like it?" I said.

A whispered surprise-freighted choke left her throat, "A gun? What are you doing with a gun? Where did you get that?" she asked.

"Oh, at Woolworth's." I shook my head for her to quiet down. "Don't worry. I know how to use it. I even know its name. It's a Walther semi-automatic 7.65 mm. We are not defenseless poor little women. Let's go. I want to find Charles."

"Oh, no. This is as far as I go. See you tomorrow, Miss Captain America. I'm going home. It's getting dark and I'm getting the creeps."

"But, you come to work here every night. What, scared?"

"Me? Yes, okay, big burly men with muscles like sledgehammers scare me. I work here, yes and the guards escort a group of us from the subway to the office. You know why? Because Hitler would love to blow this place to smithereens. That's why."

"I'm going down the alley. Just to see what's there. Come on. We haven't seen anyone around that building. Chances are no one is back there. But maybe we'll find an open door. Let's go. Don't be a sissy."

I grabbed Joann by the arm and yanked her up. Her chair fell over and banged hard on the floor. Our host jumped and just stared at us as he dried dishes. "Ladies," he said, "you should go home now. It can be dangerous here at night for strangers and you don't sound like you are from around here."

"Yes, we are about to meet our husbands in front of the Yard gate." That sounded like a safe lie.

We paid the bill, said goodnight and left.

We slipped into the darkened alley. The tall buildings on either side blocked the last rays of the daylight. I held the pistol in my hand inside my purse with my finger on the trigger as we crept along the wall, stepping over a pile of wet newspapers, but no bodies. We did find a small victory garden with overripe tomatoes and peppers. Best of all, we saw the door into the back hall of the ground floor behind the lobby yawning at us.

A single light bulb lit the passage to a short flight of steps up to the foyer. "We should have thought of this earlier. He might be dead by now and we let him bleed out."

"Oh, for goodness sakes, Joann, you're getting on my nerves. We still have to get through another door…" I tried the handle but couldn't budge it. "And it's locked."

"Marie, look. Here's Charles Stanhope's name next to the Apartment number 302." She pressed the buzzer. I hoped he would open the inner door with a buzz back, but nothing happened.

"I guess we're at a dead end. Let's go," she said and turned to leave.

Just then a woman with a little white dog on a red leash came out into the foyer from the main hall. The dog took his time walking so we had time to rush inside behind him. Joann held onto the back of my suit jacket and we climbed up the dark stairway to the third floor. The door to #302 was ajar. I pushed it open after knocking.

"Charles? Are you in there?" What a dumb question, he would have buzzed back. "Are you okay?" No answer. "Charles, where are you?" I called.

Joann murmured, "Shush, I think I hear something."

Joann and I looked at each other and nodded agreement before pushing the door all the way open. We stepped over papers and clothes strewn over the floor. They didn't even look like what Charles wore. At least not when he was with us. There was a heavy winter jacket, snow boots, a woolen scarf, and goggles of all things. The radio was playing classical music.

"Someone looked for something." I said and turned off the radio next to the sofa.

"Think so?" Joann replied with a sarcastic note in her voice. She squeezed her tired eyes shut for a moment and rubbed them. The coffee we drank at the café did not give her enough energy to continue much more investigating. I had to get her home soon. She should never have come.

The kitchen was as neat as a pin except for a half cup of tea on the table. We tiptoed into another room. A jumble of blankets and sheets covered the single bed, but no blood or bodies. I took special notice there was nothing suggesting a woman lived or slept here.

"No one wounded and no dead bodies. No live ones either for that matter."

"Whatever happened here? Doesn't look like he went to work. Here's his badge. Wait a minute. This badge says William MacPherson. Who the hell is he?" Joann asked. *Well, well, well, a new twist.*

I pulled open drawers, checking under socks, t-shirts, and boxers. "Look, a passport. The name on the passport says MacPherson, and he entered the United States three times in the last year."

Joann nudged me while I started looking for my cigarettes, found the pack and lit up.

"What do you think this means? Is he

MacPherson or Stanhope? I wonder how many identities he has." I took in a deep drag as she studied the passport picture again. I rounded up my suspicions like a ball of yarn after the cat tangled it. Then I had no ideas left.

"I don't know. This picture looks like him, but when I glance again, it doesn't look like Charles at all." Joann said.

"Maybe it is just an old picture and not a very good one," I said and stared at the eyes in the black and white photo.

"No, this is definitely not Stanhope. Here, look again. This man is younger," she said.

"Let's get out of here." I walked back to the kitchen and dashed my cigarette out in the sink, washed down the remains and turned to Joann. "I think we're done. At least I am for now." I held onto the flicker of hope of seeing Charles once more.

CHAPTER FIVE

THE SUBWAY AND BUS HOME took longer than usual.
Traffic along New York Avenue held us up. Likely
a truck ran out of fuel in the middle of the street. I
finally stepped off the bus about midnight. At the
dark, almost deserted corner a newsboy sold the
morning papers under the street light. A mist
shrouded the night sky threatening rain any minute.

"New York Daily News, Miss Gentile? Mirror,
Hudson Dispatch?"

"Thanks, Pete." He dropped the coins into the
coin changer he wore around his waist. I took a
quick glance at the front page, thinking I might see
a picture of a missing Charles Stanhope or a story
about a captured foreign agent, but the only news
was about the Russians advancing on the western
front.

I walked the two blocks home breathing in the
mist. It felt clean and cool after the stuffy bus. I
liked my building and looked forward to seeing the
familiar marble lobby and carved wooden molding

in the hallways. My heart lifted when I looked up and saw my kitchen light. Oh, Gus was home. No, no, Gus was not home! Gus was dead. He lived at his own permanent forever home. Dead and buried in Fairview Cemetery. Shot in the neck by a stray bullet in basic training. Yikes! How weird could life get? Would I ever forget to remember him? A sweaty shiver rushed up my back; I squeezed my eyes and tears flooded over. I guessed that was part of the business of the missing a loved one.

I opened my door. An arm came around my chest, a hand cupped my mouth, and a wisp of hot breath touched my neck. I pushed and pulled at the arm without success. Then a familiar accent whispered, "Don't scream, love, not going to hurt you. Stanhope here." I nodded. My arms went limp, my knees folded in the aftershock. I tried to turn around to face him, but I fainted.

I awoke and found myself sitting half in his lap. "My dear, how nice of you to meet me again," he said and I wiggled to get out of his arms and stand.

"Rest a minute, darling. I'm sorry for this frightful attempt not to scare you."

"And you are an uninvited guest at my place, Mr. Stanhope—or whoever you really are."

Charles pushed me gently aside, stood up with his shoulders back, chest out, and offered me his hand, which I refused. But, for goodness sakes, I did want his hands on me again. Those nice, strong, hands and arms. Wouldn't I love to have them touch me! I confess I did want to grab hold and pull him down close to me again, but Gus stared at me from a picture I had taken two summers ago at Atlantic City beach. I shook the memory away, kicked off those shoes, and sat leaning against the door waiting for my insides to stop tumbling from the rollercoaster ride I had been on all day.

I squinted, tilted my head up towards him, and whispered fiercely, "Forgive you? What the hell are you doing here? Joann and I thought you were dead in some alley or captured and tortured in some moldy old cellar with rats crawling over your feet. And who are you anyway? Who is MacPherson? You? How did you get in here anyway?" My fierce whisper got louder as I ranted, but he just smiled.

Stanhope or MacPherson ignored my questions and walked towards the kitchen. "Tea, coffee, brandy, whiskey?"

"Brandy would be just fine. I see you have found your way around." He brought a snifter of brandy. I purposefully touched his fingers when I took the glass just to see if a spark ignited. He stood in front of me a moment longer, a slender muscular frame, a strong neck and a 29-inch waist, not very tall, but tall enough for me. He wore a white shirt with sleeves rolled back from his wrists and gray trousers with suspenders.

We sat across from each other on either side of the silent fireplace. "Well?" I focused on his eyes without blinking and picked at the arm of my faded blue chair, waiting for an answer.

"Well, well what?" he said at last.

I got up, looked around the room as if the answer

were out in the air somewhere. Then I moved to the sofa, "Well, what are you doing here besides scaring me to death, drinking my brandy, and making yourself at home for one thing? Pardon me. That added up to three things. Oh, and one more thing. Again, how did you get in here?"

"So, what did you find today?"

Son of a bitch, he's answering a question with another question. Well, I knew how to play that game. I smiled and looked away, slowing my breath. I sniffed my brandy and looked up at him through my lashes. A warm glow took over and quieted my shivers. I got to my feet again and moved toward the bedroom. "What?" I asked. "Whatever are you talking about, stop. Listen, mister, I'm going to change my clothes and you are going to enjoy that drink and think about answering me, Mr. Stanhope or MacPherson or whatever your name you call yourself."

"Oh, I think you know what I am talking about. In the apartment you visited today, what did you find?" Charles called after me.

"Who? Me? No, you're mistaken," I called back. I went to the bedroom door to see him. "You are in my territory now. You answer to me." Listen to me. Sounding tough like the boys in the old neighborhood.

"Yes, darling, you are quite right."

The most confident, sexy guy I'd ever met sat in my very own living room staring at me as I watched him in the mirror of my dresser. He stood up. My heart thumped once or twice and I started to unbutton my blouse. He stopped and stared at me in the bedroom doorway, but then turned and walked toward the kitchen. I pulled a brush through my hair, grabbed my satin quilted robe and made sure I covered up.

I lied, "We didn't go to any apartment. You didn't show up this morning, so Joann and I went to the movies. A double feature. With popcorn. A wonderful relaxing afternoon watching newsreels of your war. We sat in the balcony and I smoked and added candy to the meal. Lovely of you to ask."

Charles knew I had lied. How did he know? He walked to the window and pulled the lace curtain aside before he said, "And what was it you found in the apartment? You know, the one near the Navy Yard, love, the Navy Yard in Brooklyn? You say you found a passport?" His voice was as smooth as the brandy.

I toyed with the velvet piping on the arm of my chair.

"Navy Yard? Brooklyn? A passport? What do you mean?" I could keep this up as long as he could.

"Charles. Please call me Charles, love."

"No, thank you, Mr. Stanhope. I will not call you Charles or any other friendly name you might prefer. That would be much too much and right now I'm not in a very friendly mood. I'll stick to Stanhope. You are a deceitful nefarious man."

What was I thinking last week when I wanted to call him something endearing? Chaz or Chuck, what a trusted friend would call him or what a girlfriend calls her boyfriend. This fellow was no such thing. He was not going to be Chaz or Chuck or Charlie to me since the passport popped up. "Just who are you really, Mr. Stanhope?"

"Stanhope truly is my surname and Charles is my given name. I shall tell you all in due time after you admit you found a passport at the apartment."

"First, tell me how do you know I was there?"

"Certainly. My friend owns the café and served you this afternoon. He informed me."

"And where were you?" I was determined he would answer me. I covered my knees with my robe and sat up very tall and straight.

"That, my dear, is for me to know and you not to know. After all, I am a spy. I cannot and will not compromise my work by answering your every question."

"Okay, so you had us watched? Why? We are just two simple girls from New Jersey. We are nobodies and how did you know we were there? Was the café owner waiting for us?"

"Yes, I had him look out for you and Joann when I left my apartment. I thought you might show up there. Marie, there are some things you may know that you don't even know you know. So I entrusted him for the time being with your safety."

"Entrusted him with my safety? But why? Anyway, I can take care of myself well enough." I stared at the picture above mantel Gus and I had bought. It was a beautiful woodland scene. Behind the trunks of white birches, leaves of red, gold, and orange filled the background where a small blurred figure of a man in a cloak walked. I imagined it to be Christ and often prayed before it.

"Oh, yes. I know you think you can. Do you

mean with the little thing you carry in your purse?"
He smiled, shook his head and went back to the
window to peruse the street below.

I laughed aloud thinking about what else he
knew about me, "Oh, my God! Oh, my God!" I
stood and paced the length of the room. "What else
do you know? The color of my underwear?"

"Well, yes, as a matter of fact. Some are pink
and others are white. I know you were in love with
a man and still grieve for him after a year. I know
you take flowers to his grave once a week. I know
the circumstances of his death."

I glanced at a photo of Gus and me on the lamp
table beside where I sat. Grief overcame me again
and I slammed my hand on the pillow in my lap.
"Don't you dare mention my feelings for Gus
again."

"A tragic casualty of unprepared men. I know
you work in your brother's law office. I know you
are fluent in Italian and French. I know you yearn
for a change, maybe even an adventure. I know you
are intelligent, with an IQ of 155. You graduated
college with a degree in political science. I know
you turned down enlisting with the WACs. I know
you attend Catholic mass on Sundays and
sometimes visit the church during the week. I know
your brother, Mario."

"Well, you can let poor Gus go and rest in peace.
I am not about to talk." I played with my fake gold
cigarette case from Atlantic City, and rose to refill
my snifter.

He followed me into the kitchen, where he put a
hand on the enamel sink and touched one of the four

59

green wine bottles with plant cuttings sitting neatly on the windowsill. "Right. My reason for coming here now at this time of night. Do you still want to know?

"Let me think a minute. Hmm... I remember now." I asked, "What the hell are you doing here? Are you really a spy or something?'"

"Yes, I am. Now as far as Mario goes—"

"Mario? What does he have to do with this?" I looked at my own hand just a few inches from his, the knuckles whitening as I gripped. This was getting complicated. What next? My mind spun, my knees weakened and my head ached. There was too much happening at once. I went back to the living room and plopped into the armchair again.

"The letters you type for him are sometimes encoded. You mail them to false addresses. Your mail boy delivers them to a contact waiting in front of the Horseshoe Bar. That man takes them directly to the 32nd Street Post Office. Another person, man or woman, empties the mail into another bag, briefcase or shopping bag, different every time, and takes it to Penn Station in New York City where she passes it to another carrier who takes it by train directly to the D.C. or wherever the President is."

"Encoded letters to the President?"

"Yes."

"But why?"

"Marie, believe it or not, your country is involved in the war. In any event, you have not yet realized Mario's office, your brother's law office where you work, is part of a network of spies and counterspies. It serves as a recruitment center for men and women who want to serve as spies. His office takes care of Europe. Your cousin's office in San Francisco takes care of Asia, Cosmo Palmieri is his name. So you see, you really work for the office of the President."

He sat on the arm of my chair. He took my shoulders and turned me toward him as he watched and waited for me to react. I stood there dumbfounded, mute as a scared rabbit. He smiled a soft inviting smile I wanted to touch with my lips. Oh my goodness, I still wanted to touch this man after all that had happened, or not happened, that day.

I said, "Why are you smiling, Mr. Stanhope. It's not funny. I don't believe you. I would have caught onto that. I may be a simple girl, but not a total fool."

"No, you are not a fool, but you are naive. We were doing everything we could to keep you in the dark while we are setting things in motion." He ran his thumb along my chin. I held my breath and pulled away, although I shivered down to my toes from his touch. I knew then I was alive and well.

"This will become very clear," he said. "Mario will be here shortly and you will know then that I am telling you the truth, sweetheart."

"Mario's coming here? It's in the middle of the night for goodness sakes." Just then I heard the front door unlock and saw my brother stride across the foyer into the living room. He kissed my cheek. What is this? Some kind of Mafia kiss of death? My own brother? I am just a secretary in his law office. These guys are what? Spies? Gangsters? Smugglers? All of the above?

CHAPTER SIX

I SHOVED MARIO AWAY WITH my two hands on his chest. "Mario, what the hell is going on? Why are you here and who is this man? I thought I knew, but now I am not sure of anything, let alone him." I was exhausted and empty of trust. I had missed the boat these two gentlemen were sailing. I had missed out on something big. There might be a chance to get back on board, but my weary bones and my emotions got in the way. My brain was numb. I didn't know what to say or do next.

Mario ignored my question. "Let's make coffee. Do you have any biscotti?" He exuded confidence as the leader in his law office, in our own family and now here in my home. Ever since we were kids. My big brother coming into my home and taking charge annoyed me to no end. Oh for goodness sakes, I thought, here I was again, feeling my poor helpless self in my brother's presence.

I took a deep breath, determined to take charge of my kitchen and of the conversation. "Sure, in the cabinet over there by the window. You can't have any until you answer me. Would you answer me, please?" I said without a breath. The kitchen became claustrophobic where two big men and I were standing in my home where I had been alone for months. I grabbed the coffee pot from Mario. "Get out of my kitchen. Go sit inside. You too, Stanhope."

I met Charles's deep blue eyes and caught my brother staring at me. Did I see his lips curl up at the corners? "Go, I'll be right there." I pointed at the doorway, ignoring him.

The two men moved into the living room and I, being the ever-gracious hostess, prepared the coffee and placed it over the flame to perk. I put biscotti on a plate and took the cups down from the cupboard.

"So," I said as I retraced my steps to the sofa, "I will speak first. *I* will ask the questions. If either of you is not going to answer, you might as well leave now and let me get some sleep. I'm tired from chasing after you today." I glared at Stanhope's smiling blue eyes and unshaven face. *What was so funny? Me?*

"Marie, listen, we are here because we have worked together. If you agree to what we offer, you will join with us to fight the devil in Europe," Mario said with a clear voice and eye.

"First, you must promise to keep secret everything we talk about tonight," Charles said. "Not even Joann is to know. We do not want to put her in any danger." He took a cigarette and paced in front of me. He scared me. He was more serious than I had ever seen him.

I looked from one to the other, then, got up to get the coffee. "Okay boys, sure, I promise, but only because you're going to let me play with you." I crossed my heart the ways kids do. This was a game I did not yet understand. Neither one cracked a smile. Mario and Stanhope just looked at each other and nodded.

The coffee was ready. Its delicious aroma filled the apartment at once, bringing me back to the fact that what was happening was real and frightening. I set it with the biscotti on a tray. Stanhope came up behind me and took the tray to the living room. After a few bites and sips of sweetness, I lost the bitter taste I'd had on finding Charles in my apartment. Nevertheless, I held my breath to keep from screaming at the two of them.

"You first, Stanhope. Who are you?" Another sip of coffee. "And stop looking at me."

"Well, I am assessing you. Mario here says you are bright and courageous. I guess if you chased after me, found the passport, you are courageous. Mario says you want to take on dangerous tasks like investigate criminal cases." He stopped and winked at me.

Mario didn't see him do it. I, on the other hand, saw myself softly kissing that winking eyelid and the other one, and the cleft in his chin, and his throat, and the bands of muscles across his chest. I pulled myself together and said, "It was a stupid thing Joann and I did today. I agree. We might have found you dead. Then what? Never mind. What and who are you?"

"I see you are headstrong and persistent." He lit

another cigarette and took a seat in the other armchair.

"And you? Will you just stop a minute and tell me who you *are* really?"

"I am actually Charles Stanhope, Lord Stanhope to be exact, although the family can no longer lord it over anyone at the moment."

"Would that be because you don't keep appointments like today?"

"You might have something there. I confess, not keeping appointments is a fault of mine. My brother, Edmund, usually takes care of those, but he is not with me at the moment. Here is the truth of the matter. It is not an unusual truth for the upper class in England to have lost their fortunes after World War I. My family lost most our holdings in what was supposed to be a sound investment in a tea plantation in India. Anyway, soon, most of the family properties had to be sold to pay off creditors. My parents have passed on and my siblings and I divided the remaining funds among us for daily expenses."

"Oh, of course. A close family! Right, Mario? Sounds just like ours. Indeed." I interjected, but a heat wave hit my tummy along with a shiver that rolled across my chest. When I looked at Charles, I sighed. I didn't want him to think I disliked him now. I gazed down into my cup and scraped the arm of the chair with my fingernail.

He sat on the sofa and stretched out his long legs. "We each took a share of what was left. We had enough money to live for a few years and a townhouse in London that we share. All four of us had to find employment, which as you can guess, was difficult with the economy the way it was." He removed his glasses and rubbed his eyes.

"Then my sister, Lydia, had a brilliant idea. My brothers and I laughed at first, but soon saw the logic. We had liked playing a cat and mouse game as children, so why not as adults? We were good at spying on people and gathering information on strangers who came near. So it seemed logical to set up a detective agency."

Charles lit a cigarette while he kept those sea blue eyes on me. I watched him, but my eyes were heavy; staying awake was becoming difficult. The long day was catching up to me. My temples throbbed. A headache brewed behind my eyes. Was it the soft blond hair on his forearms and the muscles under his shirt that so disturbed me or was it his ridiculous story?

I watched Stanhope and Mario, who was busy with the biscotti and coffee. I knew my brother well enough to know he listened to every word, but had probably heard this before.

"So? So you set up a detective agency. What does any of that have to do with me?"

"We were lucky to get a head start on the art of stealing and spying in Germany without being caught. We educated ourselves with maps and German dictionaries. Edmund bought us extra warm clothing and such for traveling on foot through Germany. We saw firsthand that Hitler was strengthening his military power, his munitions, and aircraft factories."

He paused and paced the room a few times.

Before he began again, he looked at me and I caught a glimpse of the sadness in his features. He slumped into the loose-back cushion and crossed his arms over his chest. The war had done a job on him.

"Richard, my oldest brother pawned furniture and jewelry in exchange for radios and transmitters. Lydia recruited and organized a network. By then our illustrious Prime Minister had shaken hands with Hitler. We assessed on the day Hitler invaded Poland that it would be only a matter of time before he would strike out for other European countries including England. We infiltrated Germany to learn all we could about troop numbers, movement and the ambitious Nazi plan."

"What did you do with that information? Sell it?" I sat up straight in my chair with my feet under me. I remained consumed with interest in his story.

"Not exactly sell it. We wanted to share it with the Prime Minister. We approached our government for a contract to continue the intelligence gathering, but were refused. Prime Minister Chamberlain was convinced by the liar, Hitler himself, that Germany would not invade Poland or England. No one in history has been more wrong. Anyway, by then Hitler and Mussolini were partners. The Nazis quickly occupied Denmark, the Netherlands, Norway and France. The nations were unprepared for military operations. They wanted to remain neutral territories, but were forced to capitulate."

"And you and your family?"

"We now work with the collaborative intelligence agencies of all of Europe and the United States. As we speak, Europe is hell right now. Dutch, Danes, Norwegians, Pols, Italians, anyone not of the pure Arian race is considered dangerous and expendable. Oh, yes, and the top of the list are Jews."

"Oh God have mercy on them," I whispered more to myself than to Mario or Charles.

Charles continued. "More than ever we need undercover operatives. It is inevitable Hitler will declare war on your country too."

Chills ran up my arms and they weren't from being cold. I thought of Gus's family still in Greece and my own cousins in Italy. "Your network then is one of intelligence-gathering agents. Again I ask, what does this have to do with me or Mario?"

I sickened at the thought of what his answer might be and ran to the bathroom with a burn in my belly. It flamed up into my throat right before I choked up the brandy, biscotti, and coffee. *Oh Holy Mother of God, what was happening?* My world was falling apart.

Charles was right there behind me, wetting a washcloth and putting it to my neck. He said something like "over the crapper, darling." *What was he talking about?* I sat on the floor against the wall. The room spun a few times to the right, then to the left. Whatever Charles was saying literally made me sick.

"Don't be frightened, love. You won't have to go into any of those countries. It would be too dangerous for you." He pushed my hair back from my forehead.

Mario spoke up from the doorway. *Oh my God, couldn't he just stop for a minute?* "That is why we're here, Marie. Americans and Brits are working together to form an organization of spies to be trained and sent into Europe, Asia, and Africa on intelligence missions."

"Ah, wait, not for me. I kind of like chasing cheating husbands and wives around town," I said. Charles carried me back to the living room and set me on the sofa. Mario came and kissed me on the forehead as he put a pillow behind my head.

Charles continued, "You are a perfect candidate for Italy."

"Oh, no you don't. I told you once before that this isn't my war." I took a deep drag on a cigarette thinking over his last statement. "Me? You think I could do that? No, wait. Don't answer. Obviously you do."

I tried to absorb what I had heard. Just a few minutes ago I'd looked into sea blue eyes and thought about ripping off his clothes. Now he and my only brother were trying to talk me into becoming a spy.

"Go to Italy? What would I do? Look through binoculars for Nazis and Fascists?" I giggled. "For a minute I believed you. Men! Always teasing and making fun of women. You're joking, of course."

I looked at their deadpan faces. "You're serious, aren't you? Oh, my God. Don't. Don't do this to me."

"Yes, very serious," Mario said. His face tightened with anxiety and maybe trepidation, as it should. He was trying to send his sweet baby sister to war.

Charles sat, smoking. I could still feel his arms

around my back and knees or had they been Mario's? I couldn't even remember who had carried me from the bathroom, and these two men wanted to send me overseas. *What the hell were they thinking?*

I looked at Charles's lovely face. "We need someone to translate, organize, and send reports from the field to our commanders planning the liberation of Italy," he said.

Not one of them was paying attention to the fact I was sick. I had just thrown up and they continued talking as if nothing had happened.

Mario added, "It's relatively safe. You will be far from the front line and you will be under the protection of Italian nationalists and American soldiers."

I stood unsteadily and paced in front of them a few times. "You're kidding me, aren't you? I'm not a spy. I don't know anything about intelligence gathering. You need someone like Josephine Baker, you know, the entertainer, to do this. Someone who already knows the countries in Europe firsthand."

I took a cigarette from my robe pocket. Charles held his lighter to it. This time I looked at him through my smoke. This was all too complicated and somewhat ridiculous. I just wanted to kiss him from head to toe. Why were we talking about spies?

I sat on the sofa, put my head back, closed my eyes, and tried like hell to picture myself in the white desert of Africa and the green hills of Italy. The men remained silent for a few minutes.

I heard a woman's voice say, "Okay, what do I have to do?" *Oh, for goodness sakes who was speaking?* I waited and heard her again. "I'll go. What do I have to lose? I've already lost the love of my life." *What was I saying?* Someone inside me said this was the best thing I could do with the rest of my life. I would never have Gus again. How curious. Mario thought investigating criminal cases was a man's job, but this spy thing was okay for a woman like me. Times were changing.

I spoke quietly, but definitely spoke. "Okay. I'll do it." There it was. I had agreed to become a part of…what? A spy movement? Oh, my goodness.

The three of us remained still for a few minutes. The final drops of rain were tapping the window. The storm was over, but a new life was just beginning for me. The sound of church bells calling believers to Monday morning mass broke the silence. Mario and I looked at each other. I saw him blink back tears and give me a nod. He and I knew what to do next. We washed, gathered ourselves together, and put on our coats.

"We're going to church, Charles. Would you like to come?"

"No, love, you two go on. I'll stay here and wait for you." He turned from me to Mario and offered his handshake. "Mario, thank you. You have been a tremendous help to me and dare I say, England. We will meet again."

Mario and I walked arm in arm along the wet sidewalk in the light of the morning sunrise. This was something we had done every morning as children. His strong arm entwined in mine comforted me. Our gait was slow but steady. My heart filled with an immense sense of adventure, anticipation, duty, but a lack of courage blanketed all that. I intended to pray for huge amounts of bravery.

After mass Mario walked me back to the apartment, but did not come in.

"I think you and Charles have some things to sort out so I'll go now." He took me in his arms and whispered in my ear, "Be careful, sweet baby sister. Remember how important and necessary this is."

"I know. I know," I said, impatient with him for doubting whether I understood how consequential the intelligence business was.

"Just remember who you are on the inside. You will always be on our minds and in our prayers and don't forget to go to church. *Arrivaderci.*" His stern glare warned me again to be serious. I could tell worrisome thoughts had invaded his previous confidence.

"Okay, I promise. I'll be the best student and follow all instructions—besides, have you ever known me not to follow instructions?"

"Stay in Italy if you can. When this damn war ends, Angie and I will join you for vacation."

I imagined the tall cypress lined on a sunny hillside and St. Peter's Square on a rainy day. But then again, maybe Italy would lay in ruins.

Mario told me Charles would see me off the next

morning from Penn Station in Manhattan. Someone would meet me at the final stop in Toronto and take me to the training camp.

I reached up and hugged my big bear of a brother, fighting off tears, and smiled. "No, come to think of it, England sounds better to me right now."

"Hmm." His eyes crinkled. "So, sweet on Mr. Stanhope, eh? Santa Maria, I would never have guessed." He chuckled and popped a Chiclet in his mouth, cracking it between his teeth.

"Not so," I snapped.

"Liar."

I sent him a smile. "Umm…just a little. Honestly, guilt hovers over me like a halo when I think of abandoning Gus's memory. Anyway, now, it doesn't matter how sweet I am on Mr. Stanhope. We'll be apart for God only knows how long. To tell the truth I don't know how I feel about him, but I would like to find out."

"Live your life, little sister."

"Thank you."

"One more thing. Charles isn't married as far as I know."

"Good, I guess he did tell me the truth about that."

An unexpected breath of fresh air whirled around me and I experienced a great sense of relief. Greater than anything I had felt since I buried Gus. My heart emptied itself of the bleakness of the past year. Though the war raged in the background, excitement whirled inside me. Incandescent hope rushed through my veins when I thought of the future. I realized that a new life had begun for me.

"Come here," Mario said and reached out for one last hug. "God bless you, Marie." He pinched my cheek and kissed me.

I put both arms around his neck and held tight, then patted his arm and said, "Don't worry. I'll be fine." My knees were shaking and my insides were quivering, but I saluted my brother. *I'm ready. Lord, help me.* A prayer I would say often.

CHAPTER SEVEN

ONCE INSIDE I SLIPPED OUT of my shoes and looked around. Charles had busied himself washing glasses and cups. He was stretched out on the sofa with a pile a papers on his chest. His morning whiskers outlined his thin angular features. His lips fluttered with his breath. His eyelids pulsed in front of a dream. Resisting an impulse to touch him, I pulled a blanket down from the hall closet and laid it over him before going to my own bed. Sleep came like a purring kitten.

"Evening, love." I heard from the other side of the room. "Time to rise and shine."

I peeked out with the covers over half my face. "Charles Stanhope, is that you coming out of my bathroom wrapped in a towel or am I dreaming?"

"Stanhope here in person. Come on, we have things to do. It's past seven p.m. You've slept all day." He rubbed his hair dry with another towel, which he then dropped on the floor before coming closer. Oh my goodness, his very muscular chest glistened with rivulets of water, the light from behind him bounced off his shoulders and his mouth looked wet and delicious.

"Past seven? I wondered why it's dark, but it feels like morning."

He came to the bed and sat beside me. "Very beautiful, Marie. Blond hair mussed begging to untangle through my fingers. Cheeks pink with anticipation. Lips the ripe color of cherries. Marie?"

"What?" I whimpered.

"I am falling in love with you." He ran the side of his index finger along the satin edge of the blanket. I held my breath as I searched his eyes, reached up and ran my fingers through his damp hair.

"Charles?"

"Yes?" he asked as he lowered his face towards mine.

"I am not ready for this."

"Oh, yes, you are, Marie. I would not be here if you weren't. Little touches here and there over typewritten drafts are no longer enough for me."

"Oh, did sweet goodnight kisses change to madness? You are next to me on my bed with only a towel taking the place of the dumb raincoat. May I ask your intention, Mr. Stanhope?"

"Why, are you ready now, love?" His breath touched my neck, sending electricity down to my toes. I felt like a woman again. My senses heightened. I yearned to taste the droplets of water still on his chest and some other ones.

"Is you intention to get under these covers with me?" I smiled as he stood, dropped the towel and uncovered just what I needed at that moment.

I held my breath and watch a smile appear on his mouth. I shivered with hunger for his touch.

"Oh, and you're not forward at all? Just like a man."

"Yes, so I am. All man."

"I've secretly wanted to see you in a towel instead of the raincoat since I met you. I hated every minute looking at you in that damp dark dungeon of a basement with your clothes on."

"Really? Thank you. Now what?" he asked.

I kept my hands under the covers.

"Tell me, love. What do Americans do in a situation like this?"

"What situation?" I teased.

He ran his hand through his wet hair. My heart began to bounce between my ribs like a ping pong ball, making the center of my womanhood cheer me on.

"A naked spy and a woman wearing only a film of a nightgown under the covers. The makings of a book." He came closer and I took in his clean fragrance and closed my eyes.

His little kisses melted like snowflakes on my face.

"I saw a movie where first the lady unbuttoned her nightgown and bared her shoulders. Just to equalize things, since the man is already naked as a newborn," I said and unbuttoned enough to reveal one shoulder, then the other, while his lips moved over me.

"You are lovely," he said when I touched his chest.

"Then the woman tilted her head back like this." I took a deep breath before I said, "And then his lips brushed across her chin." A short little moan escaped me as he did just that.

"Right. I understand perfectly and then?" He moved toward my décolleté.

"The man lifted his face to hers and kissed her gently on the mouth and she welcomed him with lips parted…then he slid under the covers."

Charles stretched out beside me. My heart was pounding, "Do you need any more direction, Mr. Stanhope?"

"No, love, I think I can take it from here." He reached for the packet he'd laid on the nightstand.

"Not needed… never used one… never… pregnant," I murmured.

I urged him closer than close. I was wild about his face, his shoulders, his perfectly flat tummy, his navel and the long line of blond hair leading down his midline. He reached up under my nightgown and ever so gently covered me with kisses. I moved with anxious desire for him, craving him, wanting him.

"Easy, love, I want to be here all night," he took his time caressing me until there was no holding back the torrent.

"Now. I want you now. I need you now," I said and I wrapped my arms tighter around his back and opened my eyes to fall into his magic. I was a goner. Completely and utterly gone and lost in Charles Stanhope.

We stayed in each other's arms until morning when the magic of that night ended with the harsh sound of the damn alarm.

"Time to shower, love…long and hot. The water at the camp…well, it can be cool. Showers on the ship? Navy showers, they call them. You have to soap up without water and keep the rinse time short, very short, and it's salty." He marched off to the kitchen, wearing his boxer shorts and sleeveless tee shirt.

I took his advice about a hot shower, but kept it short. I wanted to see him, talk to him, and kiss him more than the morning allowed. I dried off with the biggest, fluffiest, Turkish towel I owned and sprayed myself with *Evening in Paris* cologne, my favorite. Its soft, light fragrance lingered on my skin. I wiped the steam off the mirror and this time I saw a new face flushed and alive.

"Thank you, Lord, for the miracle of life, of change, of love from friends and family. I beg you to protect us on this next great journey. Amen." I made the sign of the cross to end my prayer.

"Oh, will you look at this delicious breakfast? Thank you," I said as I sat in front of a plate filled with eggs and toast that would satisfy the rumbles in my tummy. He had made a thin savory frittata with dill sprinkled on top. "Oh my God, I'm starving. When did I last eat? Maybe at the café yesterday? By the way, tell your friend to get a cookbook."

"Love, he's a spy, not a chef."

"Where did all this come from? I know I did not have eggs."

"While I was waiting for you, I went to the market."

"Mmm, scrumptious," I said, sipping the strong dark sweet coffee. "Too bad I didn't come back here instead. Why didn't you come to the diner? You never answered me."

"I did, but you were already gone. I checked at Joann's house, but no one knew anything and the guys trailing me were close. They caught me when I reached the church. Turned out they were from General Donovan's office in New York and needed some important information from me."

"What?"

"Well now. If I tell you, I will have to kill you and you would not become a spy. In any event they left me and went to track MacPherson in New York City. So when you were not at the diner, I wanted to see you again before I left, and I was intent on having that long conversation with you and Mario," he said and his eyes crinkled into a smile.

"Yes. You certainly did. Now that you have seen all of me, what's next for you?"

He looked at the red plastic kitchen clock. "We have to leave. I will try to see you again before you go overseas. But, in this life there are no certainties."

I locked the apartment door and handed Charles the key.

"Will you see Joann and give this to her? She and Ralph are looking for a new place. This will be perfect for them. Did you know she is expecting a baby?"

"No, I didn't know. I'm jealous and you're right. This apartment is perfect for them." His mouth closed tight and straight. He shook his head. I stood there for a moment longer before I stepped back and headed for the stairwell. The breathtaking sadness of his face unnerved me.

I stopped on the first step. "Do you think we'll meet again, Charles?" I asked with a wistful glance at him.

"I plan a reunion in London after the war. I will meet you at the airport and bring you to my townhouse to meet my brothers and sister. You will love them and they will love you back. They are quite proper English. You know, high tea in the afternoon with scones and clotted cream. I will bring you to the countryside. We will visit the old castles and I will give you a history lesson."

"I'll wear a new suit and hat and bring a ton of luggage with changes for morning, noon, and evening, and you will take me to Stratford-upon-Avon to see what's left of Shakespeare's theater. You didn't know I'm an aficionado of Shakespeare, did you? The sonnets, the plays, the times, everything."

"Yes, we will do all that and more. Then you will fall in love with me because I shall be more charming and romantic than you can ever imagine." His optimism sent me into euphoria, but did not dissolve the niggling thought about how impossible it all sounded.

We didn't talk much on the bus to New York City nor on the walk to Penn Station. The crowd of men in military uniforms arriving in the City to meet the ships that would take them overseas thickened with each step. Or was that me, slowing down, hesitating, regretting?

Other men in everyday clothes headed for boot camps or naval stations around the United States. The terminal's air filled with an odor of the darkness that lay ahead. Fake smiles abounded. Women cried and clung to their sweethearts until they heard boarding time announced. I moved quicker, keeping up with Charles. I stopped once to buy *The New York Times.*

Charles rushed me to Track 49. He boarded and waited in the empty seat next to me until the very last minute. We had locked my suitcase in my berth.

"Good-bye Charles." I gave him one last hug.

"I will not say that, but I will say, see you soon, love. Is that not what an American would say?"

I kissed his lips for what I feared would be the last time, "Yes, we shall meet again. It's in the stars," I said as he ran his hand down the side of my face.

"You are beautiful, Marie. I have never met a woman as beautiful. Be careful of those Italians. I hear they make wonderful lovers." He walked toward the door as the train bucked forward preparing for the long ride to Toronto. Then he was gone and I swallowed a cry. *None of that. I barely know the man.*

I opened my newspaper with a deep sigh to catch up on the world and read that Hitler had abandoned the siege on Moscow and the Soviets had launched a counter-offensive on December 6th, 1941. That was yesterday.

CHAPTER 8

I COMFORTED MYSELF AS BEST I could on the soft velvet-like train seat to Toronto, but it wasn't easy. I was too jumpy to sit still. My knees knocked together more than they had on the subway to Brooklyn the other day. In fact my whole body screamed with anticipation of the trip and the path I was taking. My head already ached from the noise of the engine. Fear clutched my throat while excitement exploded inside my chest. How I longed to be back under the quiet covers with Charles Stanhope where only our breath, soft words and touch by delightful intuition, where no unanswerable questions interrupted us and where only sensation guided us gently to satisfaction.

The previous night contrasted as fire to ice with what I imagined lay ahead. Today my raw nerves grated the marrow of my bones. I shivered. My hands jittered along with my knees. My lips trembled and my mouth was dry. I was a mess of nerves. What had I agreed to? Organize an intelligence office in Africa? Go to Italy in the middle of a civil, as well as a world war? In one moment my insides cried out as a child afraid of a monster under her bed and in the next I saw myself on the front page of *The New York Times* receiving a medal from the President of the United States for my bravery with the caption *The Real Miss Captain American.* Oh, for goodness sakes, why had I agreed to this espionage stuff anyway? I did not fit in this picture. Was I here because I had I been hungry to impress Charles? Mario? Myself? Did I need to prove something? Was I being patriotic or did I have a giant death wish? My brain rattled like a baby's toy searching for answers.

I leaned my head on the back of my seat and closed my eyes. Nestled among the forest of questions appeared images of Charles. Charles wearing his ridiculously oversized raincoat the first time he'd walked into the diner. Charles smoking Turkish cigarettes and watching me at the typewriter in Joann's basement, or the time he walked me home when he would push my hair behind my ear and kiss me goodnight. Attached to those memories were his most intimate touches of our last night together fading into a dream. Meeting Charles, seeing my brother again, or talking with Joann was now out of my hands. A lump filled my throat just thinking of them. Surely we would all meet again. No one could venture a guess where, when or how, but surely we would. Wouldn't we?

Or would the war claim one or all of us?

Hitler and Mussolini were wreaking havoc on Europe. The Japanese were doing the same in the Far East. Defeating the Axis powers had taken precedence now. Yes, that was the reason I'd taken this assignment. Some miserable excuses for men were choking the hemispheres and maybe, just maybe, I could help stop them. I made the Sign of the Cross and asked God to protect me and have mercy on the world. I guess I had some faith left after all.

The train jolted and rocked me back to reality just as a young woman came through the door at the last minute. She caught my attention as there weren't many other women on the train. She wore a beautiful tailored dark blue suit. Her perfect make-up set off her dark bob beautifully. In one hand she carried a suitcase plastered with souvenir stickers from foreign countries. In the other she held a round pink hatbox close to her breast and a woven picnic basket in her hand. She looked down the aisle for an empty seat. I caught her eye and she came straight toward the seat next to me.

"Excuse me, is this seat taken?" she asked me.

I shook my head, "No, no. It must be yours." I smiled at her.

"Thank you. I'm Ruth, Ruth Epstein." I shook the soft leather-gloved hand she held out to me and looked into her clear hazel eyes. She was beautiful. "Exhausted already and it is only 7:15 in the morning. I can't believe this. Just send me a pillow and blanket."

"Big night?" I asked as I took her hatbox onto my lap after she placed the basket on the seat and then pushed her suitcase onto the overhead rack.

"Of sorts. My mother talked and cried a lot. She sat on my bed all night. She wanted me to stay home and keep doing what I was doing which was reviewing the police blotter and reporting on crimes in Manhattan for the *Daily News*. She's fearful my new job may take me overseas to the war zone."

"By the looks of your suitcase, it appears you've traveled around Europe," I remarked, trying to be friendly, wondering if she was a reporter or another spy going to Toronto or both.

"Yes, I studied in Germany my junior year at Columbia." Ruth picked up the picnic basket and sat in its place. "Loved every minute, almost married a German, but my parents would never have approved. You know, inter-religious marriage, Jewish-Christian. Not a good idea. Anyway I was too young," Ruth continued on. "Still am, don't you think? I'm only twenty-four."

"Oh? I don't know. That depends." I looked down at my empty ring finger and a wave of nostalgia the size of the Atlantic Ocean washed over me like cold water. A pandemonium of emotions hit me. "I never regretted marrying young nor did I ever think I missed out on anything."

The train started. I looked out the window into the dark tunnel under the city while Ruth settled herself. I relaxed as the engine picked up speed and wondered again if Ruth would be going to the training with me? How could I find out without blurting out where I was going? I had questioned many divorcees over the last few years. I should know how to get at the truth.

"So, Ruth, where are you going so early in the morning?" That was a nice friendly question to ask a traveling mate, wasn't it? Not too intrusive, I hoped.

"Oh, me? I am going to the end of the line, Toronto. You?" She didn't seem to mind telling me. I was on safe ground.

"Well, across the border. Someone will meet me up there."

Ruth volunteered, "How perfect is that?"

"Are you visiting in Toronto?" Was I being too curious? Would she tell me to mind my own business and change her seat?

"Uh, well, I'm meeting…er…a friend. Should be fun. I haven't seen her in a while. We were roommates first semester, until I began living at home again. It was too costly for my family for me to live at Columbia. You know how that is. I had a scholarship in journalism, but not for room and board. So I commuted."

"Yes, I do understand. I also received scholarship money too, but my brother had to pay my room and board."

"Lucky. I bet he worked hard to do that," she said and took out her compact to check her make-up. She brushed her hair, too.

"Not so lucky. We didn't have any parents." I said crossing my legs and smoothing out my skirt. "Mario had a lot on his shoulders. But he came through for me as always." If I confided something personal, she might open up to me. "I've never gone as far north. Is it as cold as they say?"

"I don't really know. I've only been there a few

times during college summers. This friend and I were like sisters. But you know how it goes, after graduation back to our families, live at home with parents and try to start careers, while mom tries to find us husbands. It's all she talks about. I'm still too young for a husband."

"Oh, so I guess that you don't want to get married?"

"I can't say. I say some day, maybe. Right now I just want to get overseas and hope this godforsaken war ends soon."

"And I just want a cigarette. It's been hours since I've had one. Let's go to the smoking car. It's the one behind this one." I wanted to entice her to come with me. I needed a companion while I left my seat for unknown territory. Actually going alone frightened me. How childish could I have been? I was to become a spy. How silly was that?

"Ah, no, no thanks. I'll stay. I'm not a smoker," Ruth said.

A blast of cold air refreshed me on the metal crosswalk between the train cars and a blast of blue haze enveloped me when I opened the door to the smoker. It smelled of tobacco and men's cologne. I looked down the aisle and saw three men sitting and one standing at the bar. This was apparently also the bar car. *How nice, a drink and a smoke. Just what I need. Maybe only a club soda.* For goodness sakes, it was still morning and men were drinking Scotch.

I approached the bar where the lone stranger in a

brown suit stood. A lock of blond hair fell over his forehead. His profile reminded me of Charles. *Could it be?*

I ordered my drink and put a quarter down.

"I'll get that," he said and faced me. No, it wasn't Charles. Maybe a relative, a brother?

I stared at him. Who was he? He looked like Charles, but wasn't. For a minute my head hurt and a million pictures flashed through my mind. I recovered my wits and decided to do some detective work.

"Thank you, handsome. Do I know you?" I asked and looked straight into his eyes.

"No, I don't think so. Do I know you?" he sounded pretentious. I'm William MacPherson. Ring a bell, love?"

"Love?"

I remembered the passport Joann and I had found at Charles's apartment. I lied. "MacPherson? Are you? No, no, never mind." I took a sip of soda. "Doesn't ring a bell...sorry."

"Am I what?" he said.

"Sorry your name really doesn't ring a bell," I lied and turned my head to look out the window. *Oh for goodness sakes.*

"Are you flirting?" I wanted to suggest the very thing so I could find out more about him and Charles.

"Sure. Why wouldn't I be? You're a pretty lady. I'm a man traveling with some male friends. Are you alone or with your seat companion?"

"Oh, so you've been watching me?" I leaned into him a bit. My forearm touched his.

"As I said, you are a pretty lady and I am a man. Why would I *not* watch you?" he winked at me, just like Charles.

"I am with a friend," I said, for some kind of excuse so this stranger wouldn't think I was alone.

"Perfect. Why don't you and your friend, Ruth, join me and my friends for dinner?"

"Well, if we decide to come, we'll meet you in the dining car at five," I answered before I realized he knew Ruth. "Wait a minute. How do you know Ruth's name?"

MacPherson winked at me and turned to rejoin his friends. I sat alone with my cigarette and club soda in a seat near the door where I found an old magazine. I pretended to read, but looked over the edge to watch MacPherson and his companions. All were handsome, young and dressed in suits and ties. They seemed to be engaged in serious conversation. That was all I could discern before I went back to my seat to join Ruth.

Ruth's hands were holding the picnic basket, but her bobbing head clued me she'd fallen asleep. I was practicing my investigative techniques—in case I ever did get to visit Scotland Yard I wanted to be prepared to apply for a job. *Ha, how likely is that? About as likely as meeting Charles Stanhope again.*

I tiptoed over Ruth's knees brushing against her legs. She stirred and opened her eyes.

"Oh, I'm sorry to wake you." I said.

"Don't worry, I wasn't really sleeping, just day dreaming about what I am getting into."

"I was wondering the same thing. I just met Bill MacPherson. Do you know him?"

"You did? He's on this train?"

"Well, I just met him in the smoking car."

"Yes, he is a big smoker. Camels, I think."

"I wouldn't know." *Some investigator I was.* "So, how do you know him?" *Did she know something I didn't?*

"Actually he recruited me to do some work in Europe as I travel." Ruth said looking down at her hands in her lap.

"Well. He wants us to meet him and his colleagues for dinner. What do you think?"

"That sounds swell. Let's do it. He's a nice fellow," Ruth answered. "But I am famished now. Here, have something to eat with me."

She opened the hood of the picnic basket. I peeked inside and saw a dozen or more sandwiches.

"My mother can never resist packing this basket up whenever I leave on a trip. Go on. Have something." She offered me the basket to choose what I wanted.

"Thank you. I should eat." I helped myself to an egg salad sandwich. "Can you keep a secret, something just between the two of us?"

"Yes, what is it?" she whispered between mouthfuls.

"You said you know MacPherson. Do you know Charles Stanhope, too?

"No. How do you know MacPherson?" Ruth asked.

"Well, I met him today for the first time, but I know of him. I saw his passport a few days ago in my friend's apartment."

"Can you keep a secret?" she whispered again.

"Sure."

"MacPherson works for General Donovan, the head of war intelligence for the President. Mac recruited me to work for Donovan's group. Believe me?"

"Yes. You're going to laugh at what I have to tell you. I am going to Toronto. Whoever meets me there will take me to a training camp for recruits for the intelligence team. You're going to camp too, aren't you?"

"Oh, then yes, I do know Charles. Sorry. I lied a minute ago. I met him in Brooklyn...a handsome chap. So British...like MacPherson...kind of adorable. My friends and I went out dancing a couple of times with the two of them."

Really? "Wow that must have been fun. Did you, you know, spend time alone? I mean, private time. Oh, you know what I mean." I was whispering and wondered how many other American women, Mr. Stanhope knew. I didn't give her time before my brain went crazy.

What a jerk. I was sorry I had had such an overwhelming attraction to his Lordship. I believed he liked me. Who's the jerk? Me. Now I hope I never see him again.

My blood was boiling, my head began to throb, but at the same time, I determined to follow through with my commitment to serve my country.

"No never alone with him...wonder how many

other American women he has on this train," Ruth said. "I suppose we'll find out in Toronto or maybe at dinner."

My heart hardened. Suddenly Charles Stanhope was not the man for me. He probably put on his adorable act for every woman he recruited and I fell for it, how naive was I? Now I headed for who knew what dangers. But I had listened to my brother too. Men! I would always remember Charles's sweet lingering kisses, but dared not feel their warmth again. Too many kisses and too many touches had made me lose my mind. I stared out the window into the dreary gray clouds. All I could see was Charles in the arms of other women, one after another, each one more beautiful than the next.

Chapter Nine

THE DINING CAR FURNISHINGS GREETED passengers with delightful rose velvet café style draperies on the windows and small vases of roses on white tablecloths. That first day on the way to Albany, December 7, 1941, a rumor rushed through the train that Japan had attacked Pearl Harbor. A pall of heavy dark gloom deadened the chatter. I imagined body parts floating in the ocean. Fire stripping the skin from our young enlisted boys. I didn't know what to do or say. My stomach rolled over. My hands shook. I looked at my fellow passengers. Some lost all color, others stared into space. I heard mumbled prayers. Two men argued about why Roosevelt had not prepared better. One woman stared out the window. Tears wet her face without shame.

Bill MacPherson and his friend stood inside the

door of the dining car and escorted Ruth and me to a table set for four. The news about Pearl Harbor had deflated our excitement about enjoying each other's company and our somber little group smiled weakly at each other during dinner. No one ate or talked much, although we did manage to learn something about one another.

"Rick, where are you from?" I asked the fellow with a Harvard class ring sitting next to me.

"I grew up on Long Island, I went to Harvard, and now I work for a law office in Boston," he answered. "How about you?"

"I'm from Jersey. Born and educated, graduated New Jersey College for Women at Rutgers with a degree in foreign languages, mainly Italian. I worked in my brother's law office until yesterday." I didn't mention anything about Gus, but Rick was observant and noticed the indentation of my wedding band still noticeable on my finger. I had only relinquished the ring a day or two before.

"You were married?" He touched my left hand. I pulled it back as fast as I dare without being offensive.

"Yes, I was widowed a year and half ago by a stray bullet."

"Ah, sorry."

"Thanks. I'm ready to go on, that's why I'm here." I answered.

"Good for you." He picked up a glass of water and said, "Here, here, a toast to going on, to our futures and to the United States of America. Victory!"

"Now," MacPherson spoke up, "I just want to

give you an idea of what lies ahead for you at the camp. First you will have a physical exam to detect existing conditions that might hinder you later, such as heart murmurs or babies. Ladies, if you think nine months or so from now, just stay on this train at the Canadian border, and go back home. Europe is not place to deliver a baby, if you are living in hiding from German soldiers in a barn or worse. You will be vaccinated, inoculated and percolated."

He spoke with the same British speech as Charles, the same nose, but brown eyes instead of blue.

Ruth and I looked at each other about that last word and then at Bill. It was as if we needed his permission to laugh. MacPherson waited and looked from one to the other.

"That last one's a joke, folks. Percolated?" Then we all let go and laughed together.

"Will the four of us be together at camp?" Ruth wanted to know.

"For physicals, no…for living quarters no…for meals and training classes, yes."

"Ah, showers with women were what I was looking forward to," Rick said and winked at me.

"A bigger group of you will be together. Men and women's bedrooms are separate as I said. I'm sure you appreciate that, ladies," Bill added.

"Right," Ruth said. Now Rick winked at her. What was it with these guys? They all winked a lot.

"You'll learn Morse and signal flags codes, figure out other codes and how to use the two-way radio. You'll practice in the languages of the country you will be visiting and learn how to speak English with the accent from that country."

"Is that all?" I asked.

"Almost. As far as clothes go, you'll select a wardrobe of clothes donated by immigrants for your personal use when in the field and army issued uniforms when with the troops. You'll learn local customs and mannerisms like how to smoke a cigarette European-style. Most important, you will learn as best we can tell you, how to identify Nazi or Fascists informers and, of course, the local resisters. It is not as if they wear badges. The only people wearing badges are Jews and they're the people we are to help."

"Sounds easy. All except identifying undercover resisters and Nazis," Ruth said and took a long drink of beer.

"That is the intellectual part. Camp will be just like basic training for any soldier. You have to do everything a new enlistee does. Climb rope ladders, run a few miles with a pack, parachute from a plane, and hide in the bush for a day or two after you learn survival skills. Enough for now. I am done with the lecture. See you in the morning. I will be sleeping in my seat in the car behind his one if you need to talk."

"Thanks, Bill. I don't think I can sleep. I'm too restless right now." I looked at my companions. "Anyone up for a game of Bridge?" I opened my purse and brought out a deck of cards the conductor had given me. "I'd rather not play solitaire and I need something to occupy my mind," I said. *Instead of allowing galloping fear to occupy me.*

The four of us agreed on gin rummy. We played cards in the dining car the entire night talking little of Pearl Harbor. It was too devastating to put into words. We were numbed with shock.

In the morning the trained stopped in Albany. I called Mario from a public phone I found on a windy cold platform. Fear had taken over even with the card game. I couldn't shake it off and I couldn't admit it to my companions.

"Mario, what have you and Charles gotten me into? This is too much. I can't do it. Now the U.S. is at war. I feel like everything is falling apart. I left home without even going to the cemetery to Mama and Papa…and Gus. I didn't even get to tell Joann I was leaving." I bit my thumb through my gloves. My tears were freezing on my cheeks.

"I spoke with Joann. Charles is going to see her today and give her the key to your apartment."

"Good. It's freezing here and we're not even in Toronto. I'm taking the train back to Manhattan."

I blew my nose on the hankie with the crochet edge Aunt Millie had made for high school graduation. Just holding it made me cry more.

"MacPherson gave us the line-up of what to expect. I can't do this," I wiped the tears from my chapped cheeks. "I am not fit for any of it."

"What are you talking about? You are perfect for this kind of work. Wasn't it just last week you wanted to investigate criminal cases? This is the same except on a larger scale. I know you can do it. I wouldn't have let you go if I didn't think so." Of course, he had to say that now. How would he explain my return to Donavan or Stanhope? He would look like a fool for sending his cowardly little sister.

"You think so?" I sniffed into the phone and looked around to make sure no one was watching me.

"Yes, I do, and who knows you better than I do?" I could hear him tapping his pen on the receiver. He was being as cold and unreasonable as the weather. My own brother was sending me off to war while he sat in his cozy office. What kind of brother was he anyway? He could have been a little more sympathetic.

"Aunt Millie would want me home. Have you told her? I didn't go to see her on Sunday as I had planned. Good that she didn't know. I wanted to surprise her. Now what? One of us may die before we get a chance to say good-bye."

"No, I haven't told her. I don't want to upset her and I'm planning the right words to say. She would want to keep you home and still take care of you. Listen, a chance will come to change your mind. Go to camp, why not? You're almost there. Go. Learn everything you can. Then make another decision. Okay, baby? Listen, your assignment could be in D.C. or in New York with General Donovan. Or back here in my office."

"Really, could you make it happen? I'm scared to go overseas. I won't be any good."

"We'll see."

"Okay. Try, okay? Try hard. Do you hear me?" I practically shouted into the phone. At that moment my fear was replaced with anger.

"Yes, I hear you. Listen, be your strong righteous self. The world needs you now."

I banged the receiver onto the hook before he could try any more of those annoying rah-rah lines on me again. I didn't want to hear them. I turned around and Ruth Epstein stood behind me on that platform. She put her arms around me and we both wept. Then we gazed at the headlines. Japs Bomb Pearl Harbor!

"Come on," she said, "Let's end this damn war once and for all."

We looked into each other's eyes, nodded, and walked arm in arm back to the train. Heads held high, chins up, shoulders back like the good soldiers we were or were to become.

Ruth and I slept fitfully in our seats until the whistle shrieked when we pulled into Toronto's Union Station. I opened my eyes. MacPherson and Rick Manning sat across the aisle. They were busy folding their newspapers. Rick helped Ruth with her bundles and MacPherson came with me to the berth to get my suitcase. Instead of using the berth, I had stayed with Ruth. Someone had put a blanket over us and like sisters we held hands under it.

We gathered together on the platform and I saw Ruth about to throw her hatbox into the trash.

"No, take the hat." Rick said to her. "You might be assigned to Paris and I hear the city remains pretty much the same as before the Nazi occupation. The Germans think it is so *magnifique*."

"You're right. I heard some Parisians and the commandants throw big parties with the best foods and wines. It's peaceful on the outside," Ruth said.

"Right. Big black boots kicking Jews onto East bound trains and executing resisters. Fashion is still high in ole' Pari."

"I may wear my chapel to dinner with a commandant," Ruth said.

"I heard Coco Channel dines with German officers. Is she a sympathizer or spy? What do you think, Bill?" I asked.

"I think right now, we have to find our driver before we freeze to death."

I walked through snow flurries with the others into the station proper and out the opposite door to the curb where an old man hailed MacPherson. He led us to a dark green 1937 Chevy Coupe that would take us to camp. The old man wore a brown and yellow wool plaid jacket and a heavy green sweater under it. A wool cap covered his head down to his bushy gray eyebrows. His pant legs were tucked into fur-lined boots.

"Thanks, old man, kindly unlock the boot while I gather the baggage," MacPherson said to the driver as they shook hands.

The old guy stared at him with blank eyes.

"Come now. You know what I mean, old man." Bill clapped him on the back.

"Yes, sir," the old fellow saluted MacPherson

with a chuckle. "Boot, rubber, boot, trunk. A dilemma for sure."

"Everything fits, sir, except the picnic basket and the hat box."

Ruth said, "I'll carry one on my lap. Marie, will you take the other?"

We sat in the back seat with Rick crushed between us like a frog with his knees bent up to his chin. He was much too big for this transport, but quite handsome with his fine features prominent in the dim interior light.

"Don't worry, Rick," Ruth, said, "We'll unfold you." Then she nudged him with her elbow and he growled with a very ungentlemanly smile.

"You ladies, are you comfortable back there? How about you, *oui*? You okay with the lovely ladies touching your sides?" the driver said as he threw a blanket across our laps. "Can't get the heat up much."

"Thank you, sir," Rick said. "We're all just fine. Lovely, in fact. I have always wanted to be crushed between two women, if you know what I mean?" He flashed a mischievous grin this time and winked. Again a wink, oh for goodness sakes.

"Ruth, one of us should have gone in the other car," I said enjoying Rick between us.

"Oh, now you say that," Rick moaned, as the cars pulled away from the station. "It's supposed to be a short ride. Right, Bill?"

"Yes, quite short, just an hour or two."

"Good. I'll just tuck myself in." Rick said, banging his forehead on his knees. "Well, onward."

We rode more than two hours to Omemee, Ontario before we turned onto a gravel road where the ruts were almost as deep as the tires and packed with ice.

"Rick, comfortable back there bouncing between two lovely ladies? Hope they are not crushing you to death?" Bill teased.

"Oh, just wonderful. I want more. It's a panacea for fantasies." Then he added, "I'll never mind sleeping alone again."

"Good boy," Bill said.

"He really has been a good boy. He kept his hands to himself the whole time."

We approached a gate between two trees. Black letters on the slats of the gate read Camp Whitehead. Furious snow not only buried the road ahead, but muffled the sounds from the car on the gravel. The haunting wind blew like a banshee. It was an ominous night. The fluffy flakes had changed to a blinding storm.

The driver beeped the horn and a soldier came out of the little guardhouse to check with MacPherson. It didn't take but a minute before the snow and forest closed around us, making us little bugs traveling in a giant forest of trees and wind.

An hour later Rick was still squashed between Ruth and me when a monstrous three-story building

loomed in the headlights. Rick nudged me. I looked
at his pale face and fingers tightened on his knees.
His new gray tweed overcoat and leather shoes were
as out of place here as my stocking and pumps. I
looked into his deep brown eyes and at that moment
I understood we headed for the unknown. I put my
hand on his and Ruth's covered mine.

Two Army officers in heavy winter coats opened
the car doors before we had a chance, reached
inside and lifted Ruth and I over the snow to the
warmth of the building foyer. Rich unfortunately
had to hike it.

Ruth's nerves got the best of her. She chattered
about nothing much to MacPherson in the foyer
while we waited to sign in.

"I'd love to have a German Officer invite me, a
Jewess, to dinner," she said.

He looked at me and rolled his eyes.

"Imagine Ruth wanting to be asked to dinner by a
Nazi. Would be wonderful," MacPherson said. "You
would be in a very dangerous situation. Suppose he
wanted more than dinner? What would you do?"

"What if he fell in love with me? What if he
found out I'm a Jew? Would he kill me then and
there with his silk scarf around my neck? Would he
love me enough to protect me or would he put me
on an eastbound train to a death camp?"

"Which do you prefer?"

"Ruth, stop. You're scaring me. I don't want to
think about anything like that now. Let's have some
fun while we can. Happy thoughts, you hear me?
Only happy thoughts. We are going to win this war
and we'll all be coming home."

Camp Whitehead occupied hundreds of acres small lakes, rivers, streams, cliffs, trails, hills, and well, as a valley. The lakes and streams lay as still as white marble. The cliffs and mountains pushed their white fingers into the gray sky. Sometimes it was like a fairyland and sometime like hell freezing over.

The frosted glass window on the door to our room read, *Ladies Only.* We opened it and it slammed against the bunk bed pushed against the wall. Beyond the bed on the same wall a sink and a makeshift shower where another sink had been. Hot and cold water pipes ran up the tile wall from the sink to a horizontal bar connecting them to a showerhead. A round curtain rod without a curtain surrounded the shower space. Opposite that wall were two cubicles with the toilets in tack. We each had a toilet. How considerate of the maintenance department. They really thought about privacy, but we used one cubicle to hang and dry our clothes.

"Marie," said Ruth the next morning, "the thermometer outside the window says five below. The guys downstairs promised January will be colder."

"The snow and ice make this place appear tranquil compared to the ferocious hearts of the men inside," I said.

"You should be a poet, Marie. What are you doing here?"

"Me? I plan to kill Mussolini and Hitler. That's why I'm here. No doubt about it."

"Right. Come on. Breakfast is waiting for us," Ruth said as she pulled on a pair of men's fatigues and wrapped a fine leather belt from her suitcase around her waist to hold the pants in place. She rolled up the cuffs six inches to avoid tripping. "I have got to find a pair of scissors."

"Yes, you do. Almost ready," I said from the inside of a heavy wool sweater I was pulling over my head. It had been issued to me on arrival along with thick wool socks and long underwear. I laced my boots and we headed for the mess hall downstairs from our little third floor room.

"Yea, scrumptious powdered eggs, toast and coffee," I said as we opened the door to the mess hall.

Catcalls and whistles greeted us, the only women at the camp.

"Hey, baby, come here."

"Luscious lips, I need you, darling!"

"Morning, boys," we said every day as we maneuvered our way through the food line.

"At least we know what to expect here. No surprises about food or company." Ruth answered with a happy note, nodding toward the young soldiers smiling at us.

"Hmm…Smells like bacon too this morning or is that something for dinner?" I asked. "What do you think?"

"Bacon, definitely bacon, see?" She pointed to

the steam tray holding the meat. "My father should never know I am eating pork. He would think I'm losing my faith."

I said my own little prayer. "God bless this food and all the men and women who have prepared it and those who eat it, and please keep America safe, most of all keep us safe. Amen."

With eyes closed Ruth prayed over the food in Hebrew and added in English, "Forgive me, Daddy. Forgive me, God."

"He wouldn't hold it against you in this situation," I said, then changed the subject. "You know, I'm feeling much stronger these last few days. I'm sleeping better too. Must be the exercise."

The Army recruits who manned the camp guard towers during the day always stood in line before us.

"Morning ladies," with big smiles. "I waited for you in my bed last night, but you didn't come and neither did I," one of them teased.

"Morning, girls," we said back. We called them girls. They loved it.

"I waited up for you all night, you never showed," one said.

"Will they ever mature?" Ruth giggled. "Oh, you're so cute." She said to them.

We found a seat near the outside door where the wind blew in around the frame.

We gobbled our breakfast. Ruth took a paper from her pocket, "This morning we're working out in the gym. Early afternoon decoding will highlight the day and later a volleyball game. Tonight is a class in…general European daily habits? What the heck?" she frowned and wrinkled her nose.

"What habits are you talking about?"

"You know, it's how to eat with your fork in your left hand. Gestures carry different meanings in different countries. Remember, Bill talked about that stuff."

I swallowed my last drop of coffee when the commander's young secretary tapped me on the shoulder.

"Excuse me, ma'am, Marie Gentile?"

"Yes?"

"You have a phone call. You can take it in the corridor inside that door next to the kitchen."

I looked at Ruth, shrugged my shoulders, and said, "Must be Mario."

"Oh, can I talk to him, too? I love lawyers. They are usually so correct and mature," she whispered, smiling, as she eyed the recruits.

"Ruth, I told you he's happily married," and I rolled my eyes. "But be careful if you ever see him. He is not above flirting Italian style."

"Marie? Is that you?" The British accent I'd adored until a few weeks ago confused me for a split second.

"Oh for goodness sakes. Charles, where are you?" I swallowed a lump of sarcasm with those words.

"I thought I would never get through. How are you?" His voice was low and moody. I could tell he was smoking. He brought back memories and for a second I longed to be close enough to inhale him, smoke, and all, just one time.

"Oh, just hunky dory. You know what that means don't you? Camping like the Girl Scouts do. It's just a big vacation up here since Pearl Harbor."

"Of course, perfectly understandable. Mountain climbing, carrying a backpack of gear…although it must be lovely scenery."

"Oh, really, where are you anyway? I thought you were going back to London weeks ago. Still recruiting women spies?" A teaspoon of vinegar wouldn't hurt much, but he didn't catch on and I wouldn't believe anything he said after hearing about him in Brooklyn with other women.

"I am leaving tomorrow. After Pearl Harbor Donavan asked me to remain somewhat longer to bring in more agents for the Pacific."

"And did you sleep with them, too? Or just talk them into serving their country after a few drinks?" I asked, with a cup of vinegar this time.

"What? What are you talking about, love? The recruits? It would be him not her and no, of course not even if he were a she. Marie, what's going on? I don't do that with anyone but you and I don't talk anyone into serving. The people I recruit want to serve as you do. Really love, you don't know me very well yet. Maybe we can fix that soon."

"Oh, I don't know what made me think of it. Experience. Gossip. Who knows? Some people here think you are quite the man about town. I was just wondering if you charm all recruits the way you did me. Oh, never mind, we didn't make any promises, so seeing other women is okay with me, Mr. Stanhope."

"Oh? You think I charmed you? Here I thought

you charmed me," he said lightening my mood a little. He hesitated and then, "You were quite bewitching sitting in front of the old typewriter, so dedicated, quick, adorable and...loveable."

"Really, adorable and loveable? You could melt the heart of a polar bear, Stanhope."

"Yes, really. Marie, don't think poorly of me. You are breaking my heart."

"Well, I'll say I will keep an open mind. Maybe you'll be able to sneak onto my good side again."

"I would like that. As far as recruiting women goes, I must find out what makes them tick, so to speak. See how observant and courageous they are...how they react under pressure...how intelligent and streetwise. But, be assured, love, only you brought me to bed and made me lose my senses. You are very special to me. Believe me, when I say I fancy only you."

I wanted to cover up my sharp tongue. I didn't want to be angry anymore. *What should I say?*

His charm and my memories from our first and last night together melted away my decision to stop thinking about him. But, no one here at camp, not an Ivy Leaguer, general or enlistee attracted me the way Charles Stanhope did. I put my suspicions aside. Charles Stanhope was irresistible at that moment.

"Oh? Thank you, Charles. I was just playing."

Then, I whispered into the mouthpiece with a heaping tablespoon of sugar this time, "I do miss you. And I'm glad you called. A light in these short dark days of Canadian winter, for sure."

"One more thing, love, remember, we did make

one promise to meet in London after we win," he said.

"Yes, I remember. As soon as I know Hitler's dead, I will tell you an exact date…that is…if you're still available. Will you write to me before then?" I asked. "Do you know my address? Where can I send something to you?" I began to think I would not see him ever again.

"I know where you will be, love. I will contact you when I can," he said.

"And Charles, will you get in touch with Joann and tell her something of my whereabouts?"

"No need to worry. Mario spoke to her. She has your Post Office Box. So she can write to you. That is all we can say to her."

"Good." I said. *So why hasn't she written?* I hoped she was all right. I hoped the baby was all right.

"Right, I will try to write, but I shan't until I get back from Germany. I must go now. Merry…"

The line went dead, but I held onto the receiver. I wanted to listen to that voice a moment longer. *Oh, for goodness sakes.* I snapped out of my short-lived reverie. Then Ruth hung the receiver back on the hook.

"Ah, ha. I caught you. From the look on your face that could not have been Mario."

"No, just an old friend. A charming old friend, a handsome lovely friend, a gorgeous man," I said and twirled around the cold hallway. I had to stop thinking about Charles so I could focus on my work here and abroad.

My life changed at the speed of light and I had to

keep up with more camp work and more people than just Charles, for now anyway. But, oh how I longed for his caress and his tender kisses. As many as our kisses were, I wanted more and I obsessed over Charles during those weeks at camp. We had spent only one night together, but he definitely had me. He permeated my senses. At night before falling asleep I could still feel his breath next to my ear and his fragrance surrounding me.

I still imagined him dressed in the shabby raincoat as he entered the diner or clothed in only a towel in my bedroom with his hair mussed from the shower.

What had happened to my memories of Gus? They grew dimmer and fainter as the month marched towards winter.

Christmas was that week. I wanted to lift my spirits as well as those of everyone at camp. I posted a note on the bulletin board of the mess hall announcing a meeting for those who wanted to make Christmas decorations the next day after lunch. Eight men and four women came along with Rick and Ruth.

"Okay, welcome to Christmas," I said over the hubbub of my little group and then they cheered.

"Glad you came. Would you like to decorate this place?"

"Yes, ma'am," the young officer from the guardhouse at the gate answered for everyone.

"Okay, first we have to search this building for

supplies. We need paper, any kind you can find. We need scissors as many as you can borrow…some glue or tape too. You have 15 minutes to scour this place. So three, two, one, go."

"Yes, ma'am," Rick stood up, saluted me, started to clap a beat, and said, "Let's go gang. Hip, hip, hip."

"Sir?"

"Yes?" Rick answered.

"That would be. 'Hup, hup….sir."

"Thank you, Mister, er…. Never mind. Let's go."

They rushed into the halls, knocked on office doors, and went to the third floor to the dorm rooms. They carried back whatever paper they could find including newspapers, magazines, paper towels, Kleenex and the other supplies we needed to cut snowflakes, paper chains, angels and cardboard boxes to construct nativity figures and Santa Claus.

We decorated the fir tree in the middle of the circular driveway, every door and the entire mess hall. On Christmas Eve our little group grew with more guys and gals joining us around the tree to sing carols. Christian or not, about fifty of us including Ruth joined in the singing.

We held hands and sang our hearts out. An army man took out his harmonica and we sang some songs made popular by Bing Crosby. Some guys started dancing with each other and others joined them with the ladies.

The war raged in Europe. Now that America had been forced into the fight, we tightened our togetherness and our resolve to win the war on Christmas Eve, 1941.

CHAPTER TEN

January 1942

"OUCH, MY CHEST IS BURNING." Ethel leaned over to catch her breath.

"Come on, girl. You may have to do this in the mountains of France. We're almost done. Only another mile to go," I said to Ruth. "It's easy here, no Nazis chasing us."

"Imagine running for your life in the Alps. This is just Ontario."

"You're right. Okay, let's go," I said as I took off ahead of her. This was the graduation run, the last run before the end of training the next day.

That afternoon we had our last go round on the weapons range. You would think I'd have trepidation because of the way Gus had died. I didn't. I just went ahead with my job without as much as a tear. I had transformed from a tearful widow to Miss Captain America. My heart was in winning the war as much as Charles's.

I awoke that night to loud knock on our door. Charles? No, it was the commander.

"Sir?"

"Marie, you and Rick, get out into the forest with this map and coordinates. Set explosives and sabotage the train bridge across the valley on these here grounds. Intelligence tells us box cars loaded with Nazi ammunition will cross there at five a.m." This was the final test for us, a test on explosives and sabotage.

Rick and I met in the hallway five minutes later and headed out. We hid in the forest as we made our way to the bridge. It was a cold clear night with a full moon. We had no problem reading the map and finding the site, but it became a problem staying undercover when the forest thinned. Enemy troops could be hiding anywhere. We had to stay under the cover of the brush as long as we could.

"Damn that moon," Rick said as it came from behind a cloud. "The enemy will catch us if we're not careful."

I put my finger on my lips to indicate no talking. From then on we used only hand signals to communicate. Passing this test depended on setting the charges, actually blowing up the bridge and not becoming a prisoner or a corpse.

I saw the bridge through my new night goggles

and pointed in its direction. The goggles were amazing and we were some of the first to use them. Rick and I moved from the shadow of one evergreen to another each time the moon passed behind a cloud. Then as it hid its face for the last time, we crawled the fifty feet to the bridge. Once underneath, we put the explosives in place without risk of capture. I dragged the wire with us back to safety and plunged the trigger. Right after the sky lit up with red and orange flames, fragments of wood showered the landscape. We dashed back to the commander at headquarters.

"Congratulations on your success." He shook our hands and then said, "Have a good night's sleep." What was he talking about? It was 5:40 in the morning. "See you at breakfast."

We had learned and practiced everything MacPherson had lined up. My final report read: Guns and ammunition: Excellent, remarkable shot when under stress; Character: self-determined and encouraging to others. Foreign Language: good understanding of Italian customs, language, religion and the Mafia in Sicily. Observant: astute at the workings of organizing an office. Decoding: outstanding.

I woke up the next morning in a fright when someone burst through our door, "Rise and shine, ladies, here are your graduation presents."

"Mario," I yelled and jumped from the upper bunk onto his back as I used to as a kid. He dropped his shopping bag from one hand and a box wrapped in Christmas paper from the other.

My hands were around his neck hugging him as

117

he spun around trying to shake me off. I slid off onto to Ruth's bed.

"Oh my God, they call this a living space? I don't believe it. Why didn't you complain?" he said in his grumpy authoritarian voice.

Always trying to take charge. That was Mario.

"You big dummy. You don't complain here. So stop right now acting like you can fix everything. It's our room and we love it, right, Ruth?"

I jumped into his arms and hugged him again. "Is Angie with you? Where is she?" I looked out the door, but no one else was there.

"No, no. She must not know the whereabouts of the camp," he said. "Besides she definitely doesn't like to travel...in winter of all times."

"And you want to move to Italy after the war? How are you going to get there? You think she'll go for it?" I teased my only brother who had tortured me through childhood and I enjoyed it.

"No, but it's a nice-a dream, as Aunt Millie would say, no?" He gave a big belly laugh, remembering my mother's sister. She had died while I was at camp. I never had a chance to say good-bye. The only family we had left now was each other.

"Now. Hup, hup, come on, get dressed, and come down to the mess where we can enjoy these bagels." He lifted the shopping bag to Ruth. "They are especially for you, but you can't have them unless you share."

Ruth and I looked at each other. She clapped her hands like a child with a new toy. "So you must be Mario. I'm Ruth. I guess you don't want powdered eggs with toast and coffee and you want these back and I thought they were all mine," she teased Mario. "I promise I'll bring the whole shopping bag downstairs," she said and kissed him.

Mario went down to the mess while we washed and dressed in our Sunday best. Long muddy green pants, sweaters and double socks.

I opened my Christmas gift. "I knew it. Ruth, I knew it. Two pairs of silk stockings. Here we go, one pair each. Let's wear them now with skirts. The boys have never seen us in skirts. They'll love it. We will put on a show."

I gave Ruth a pair and we changed into our traveling suits showing off our legs, making sure our seams were straight. "The boys haven't seen legs in months. They'll get a kick out of this."

"They are going to go crazy," she said. "Let's give them a show. Put on some make-up and put your hair up on top of your head."

We sashayed into the mess hall. It only took a second or two before someone noticed us. Applause and catcalls erupted. The noise only grew as we circled the tables and sang: Give me a little kiss will you, hon?

We gave the guys a great show. We posed as calendar girls like Betty Grable, with one hand on a hip and the other on the back of the neck as we looked over one shoulder. Sometimes we drew our skirts above the knee. We even dared to put one foot up on the wooden benches to show some more leg. Some of the men had cameras, but sadly they had to turn the film into the administration to archive in a vault because it identified us as Americans.

The mess crew had outdone themselves and prepared a special breakfast making pancakes along with the powdered eggs and coffee in honor of the graduates.

We shared the bagels with the grads and they cheered Mario while the new trainees jeered in fun because they didn't get any. This meal was our last before getting our separate assignments. There was some sadness attached to this graduation as to all others.

The commander called our names, shook our hands, and handed us an envelope with our orders. Rick came to our table and kissed us each goodbye. He was off to France. Mario shook his hand and patted him on the back. "Good luck, son."

"Thank you, Sir," Rick said with an anxious smile.

Ruth said, "I'll be joining Rick. We're assigned to the same cell outside Paris in the rural area."

"Where are you going, Marie?" Rick asked.

"Eventually to North Africa. Then hopefully the troops will be able to move into Sicily and then the rest of Italy. I can't wait to leave." I said to everyone at our table. "But I haven't received official orders yet."

"When does the commander think you'll head out?" Mario asked.

"So far, by the end of February. It's a wait and see situation. In the meantime I'll stay here and teach the Italian classes."

"I don't understand. The German Afrika Korps has been in North Africa since last February. The Brits are fighting there. The intelligence reports the situation as wretched. I would think we could help them out a bit and then move on to Italy," Mario said.

"Mario, dear, you know we just follow orders. Neither you nor I are in charge," I said. "I will serve where and when I am asked to serve. Now…what will you do?"

"I'll go back to my office and do the same. Wish I were the President. Oh, by the way, Angie and I planned a program to help refugees. She decided to work with parishioners of Our Lady of Grace by collecting children's clothing and sending them to the refugee camps here in the U.S."

"What camps? I didn't know we had any? What are you talking about?"

"I've been in touch with our cousin, Cosmo, in San Francisco. He said the Feds are rounding up Japanese-Americans and shipping them off to internment camps. We have to see their freedoms are protected for these innocent people as well as for the rest of us. It's for their own good. There is a lot of hatred out there for the Japanese."

"Oh, my God, you really mean protect us from them, don't you? Japanese-Americans? Has everyone gone crazy? They're Americans." I sighed. "I am so glad I didn't vote for this President. What is wrong with him? Didn't he see the signs? Lots of other people did. What a fool."

CHAPTER ELEVEN

February 1942

THE MORNING AFTER GRADUATION I met with the Camp director to set up the Italian review classes. The end of January at Camp brought more snow and ice. Every needle of every pine tree wore a coat of snow. The frozen lakes moaned and cracked like old bones with faces lined with blue veins. I dressed in layers—boots and a thick muddy green woolen army coat reached my ankles for the walk to my classroom across the quad. Going out into the cold always shook my stomach, and a burning fear settled into my throat every morning when I thought of leaving this place in few weeks. This place was safe compared to Italy.

I met with the camp director, Thomas Keating, in his smoke-filled office to discuss rules for the next group of recruits in my Italian review class. I wanted to be sure of his support.

"Sir," I began, "we have to insist every student speak only Italian in class from the get-go and every time they meet classmates throughout the day."

"Great idea. Mrs. Gentile. What do you say if we reserve a table in the mess hall where you and the recruits can eat together to maintain the practice? I'll do that for the other languages too." He surprised me with his enthusiasm and good mood so I dared to request more.

"How did you know what I was thinking? One more request, sir, can you arrange they room together? Then they can speak Italian to each other there and help each other with their family dialects." I could barely contain my own excitement. I was sure he'd agree.

"I'll do the best I can, but I can't promise. Other instructors want certain students to room together, too."

"Sir, they have to have as much interaction in the foreign language as possible and..."

He cut me off. "We all have to work within the parameters, Mrs. Gentile. You understand, I'm sure."

I faced him straight on and lifted my chin. "Yes, sir, Miss, sir. I'm Miss Gentile, but...." Ouch, disappointment hurt. I wasn't used to being denied. My brother had always indulged me. Gus had too.

"I said I would do the best I can, didn't I?" he repeated. I saw his impatience. "You will do well in the field, Marie. You are persistent, but you have to take no for an answer, especially from your superiors."

"Yes, sir. Thank you. So, when will I meet my

group?" I picked up my bag to leave with a polite but cool smile.

"They're due in Toronto this morning, should be here before dark," he said as he shuffled papers on his desk, picked up, and lit a cigar from an ashtray on the two-drawer file cabinet behind him. "You'll meet them tomorrow first thing after breakfast. That'll be time enough." He assumed a dismissive attitude.

"Good. May I see my classroom now?" I crossed my arms.

"Sure. The sergeant outside the door will take you there. I'll stop by tomorrow to see," he reassured me as he blew smoke rings above his head. "What do you plan to do for the rest of your day after the two hour class is over?"

"Me? I thought I would practice decoding some messages. Sergeant Miller said he had room in the afternoon class. Okay with you, sir?" I asked with no hope at all of getting his agreement. He had lost the good mood.

"No problem at all. Practice all you can and study the code books."

"Of course, sir."

"And don't forget to keep up with the physical fitness activities and the use of your weapon. Make sure you run every day with the new trainees and workout in the gym.

Charles Stanhope became a figment in the past. Any longing I had for him faded as his name came up now and again with words like ladies' man, man-about-town and all around cad. I had not heard from him since that phone call back in December. Stupid me had been taken in again and admitted I missed him. What an idiot I was, since I'd joined the widow's club, allowing the first man who showed me any attention to get in my bed. Well, good luck and good riddance, Mr. Stanhope. See him in England? No, I didn't think so. Not after the war, not ever. Not on his life.

Right, I didn't think about Charles Stanhope. No, I didn't really. Not much anyway. I didn't dream about being in his arms again. No, not too often. Nor did I even remember the last time we were together. Only every night. I kept myself from talking about him and hoped I hadn't called out his name in my sleep. My new roommate hadn't said and I didn't ask.

I stayed at the camp for a year. My last class of recruits was comprised of the best and most intelligent and daring young people I had ever met. The brightest lights in the entire camp so far.

"Buon giorno, (good morning)," I greeted Berdie Grossman, Christian Sapolino and Sophia Graziasini when they entered the classroom with a happy-go-lucky frame of mind. We had a few weeks together studying maps of Italy, the major dialects, the train system, geography and the political history, but the war was heating up, intelligence gathering was at the top of the priority list and our class was shortened. It didn't matter, for their Italian was the best I had heard.

My students graduated in January and I finally received my orders to meet the troop ship Verizon in New York on February 19th. Trepidation followed me like a puppy dog as I planned my departure for Europe. I was bound for Liverpool, England on a troop ship. From there I would be transported to Italy, the manner of which I didn't know, yet. I hoped I would have to travel through France

In the days between leaving Ontario and boarding ship, I returned to Fairview to my brother and Angie and of course, Joann and Ralph and the new baby. Mario met me at Penn Station and we took the bus to his house where I stayed until I was to board ship.

No sooner had I unpacked than the doorbell chimes echoed throughout the house.

"I'll get it. It's Joann with the baby," I called to the kitchen as I ran down the stairs from my bedroom.

I couldn't wait to see them and get my hands on the baby, Ralph. After I gave Joann and a big plaid bundle a hug and we squealed like we had as kids, I brought the bundle to the sofa where I uncovered the most beautiful angelic face in the world.

"Oh my, and who are you?" I cooed and kissed his little nose and his chubby cheeks. "He looks like you…beautiful little man. He has the most darling little face. And those eyes, dark eyes…dancing around under his beautiful long lashes. A real ladies' man for sure. Look, he's smiling at me. Yes, you can flirt with me, little guy." I put my cheek to his. "I'm all yours."

"He looks just like Ralph to me," Joann said and laid her coat and hat on the chair.

"No, like you. I think he looks like you. He has stolen my heart already. Haven't you?" I said and tickled him under the chin.

"He has? What about Charles Stanhope?"

"Who?" I pretended not to hear her, but I had. Even my heart had skipped a beat.

"Charles Stanhope. The Brit."

"What about him? I haven't heard from him in over a year. Have you?"

"Er…no…not heard from him. He hasn't been at the Navy Yard either. I just thought you might know something."

"Well, I can't say I haven't thought about him, only every day for a few months then less and less. I have not heard from him since last Christmas. Hope he's alive." I bit my lip. "He said he was going to Germany."

Angie came into the living room and went straight to the baby. "Ah, God bless this boy. Oh, he's got so big, Joann. Mamma mia." She kissed his forehead and his tummy. He giggled and gurgled. "I go back to kitchen to make dinner. Ralph, he's coming, no?"

"Yes, he'll be here soon."

Angie cooked a big Italian meal. She did not disappoint me. She prepared a beautiful antipasto, deep lasagna with meat sauce, breaded chicken, broccoli rabe, and of course a green salad with oil and red wine dressing.

When Mario and Ralph came, we all sat down to eat while little Ralphie slept on the floor wrapped in his blankets. We didn't want him to roll off the sofa.

The door chimes rang again. "Marie, would you get that?" my brother said and he picked up the antipasto dishes. "Must be the newspaper boy collecting for last week."

"Sure," I grabbed my purse to get change and went to the door.

"Hello, love." Charles Stanhope in the flesh was standing there in front of me. I froze for a moment and then turned, leaving the door open and walked back to the dining room with tears streaming down my face.

Mario jumped up and came to me. I think I heard Ralph say that I looked pale. Angie just stared.

Joann said, "What's wrong, Marie. You don't look well."

I whispered, "It's Charles Stanhope," and fainted into Mario's arms.

Someone waved to me from a ship. No, that's not right. Someone called me on the phone. No, that wasn't it. Someone's warm hand caressed my face. It was my Aunt Millie. No, that wasn't it either. It was Charles talking to me. What was he doing here in my dream?

I opened my eyes. His face was very close to mine. "Charles?" He looked a lot thinner than the Charles I knew, but he had the same eyes and that lock of blond hair and his wire-rimmed glasses.

"Charles, what are you doing here? Where have you been? I thought you might be missing in action or something. Mario didn't know anything either."

"Just another war story, love. Don't worry, now. This part is over for me. My brother was found out and we had to be smuggled back to England."

"Oh, my God!" I lifted myself up and reached around his neck, embracing him while he kissed my brow, my cheeks and then my lips.

"I'm sorry. Marie. I had no way to get a message out. We were with German troops on the eastern front, gathering and sending intelligence messages to MI6 in London."

"How did you do that? Never mind. I don't care about that." I kissed him again.

He lingered with me before we stood and went into to the dining room. They had waited for us before eating the rest of the meal. Angie had set a place for Charles next to me. I felt like I was watching a movie and it was about me.

I watched characters and the hero—the star—talking, but the words were only sounds all run together without meanings. I floated outside my body and after taking a few sips of wine I landed safely in my chair. I ate some.

Suddenly life was moving too fast and I couldn't keep up.

"This was fabulous, Angie. Thank you. You too, Mario," Ralph said as we sipped our demitasses and ate the last of the cannoli, "but, we have to get Ralphie home and to bed."

I hugged them both and kissed the baby about a hundred times before I let them go. Charles and I stayed until the Chianti bottles were empty and then left together.

I heard Angie say, "Modern couple, no?" as they closed the door behind us.

The temptation to turn around on the gangplank and call Mario to come haunted me, but the need to persist won out as I stepped onto the ship. A young sailor took my duffle and walked me through the caverns of the ship to my living quarters.

"Oh, my goodness, six of us in this tiny space," I heard a familiar voice say as I entered the cabin and saw Berdie, one of my last students, fighting with a gray locker door. "Impossible."

"How lucky can we get having a friend for a cabin mate. Hi, Berdie," I said.

She stood up straight, stared at me until I climbed over a small trunk in the middle of the compartment and gave her a tight hug around her slim boney shoulders.

"Oh, I'm so surprised and glad to see you. I didn't know we'd be traveling together. I didn't think we'd ever meet again and here we are among the first to sail to the British Isles." She held me tight for a moment and I felt her tremble under in my arms.

"Correggio, (courage)," I spoke softly in to her ear. "Come on, sweetie, introduce me to our mates."

Six living in one cabin for fifteen days was a challenge I will never forget. We took turns at a tiny sink to wash in salt water. We had to sleep in swaying two by six feet hammocks strung three high from the pipes, same as the troops on the rest of the ship. At least we had some privacy, the men didn't even have compartment to share.

"I heard there are about five thousand soldiers on this ship, and they sleep in big open areas on the different decks. Rows of hammocks, trunks, duffels, and metal helmets."

"I say this is better than most have. At least we have a bit of privacy," Marilyn Logan said. "The one on top has to sleep sideways to avoid getting a broken nose on those pipes up there. The ones in the middle and on the bottom have to lie according to the indentations of the one above her so as not to suffocate."

"We better not rotate in order to accustom ourselves to the contours. You know, the hammocks will retain our shapes, top to bottom and all that," Elsie Donna added.

We looked at her dumbfounded for a moment then laughed.

"Thank you, I am trying to be funny," Elsie said with a bow.

"Rock, paper, scissors. Loser taking the top." I joked, but we played anyway. It turned out it really didn't matter. We were all uncomfortable every minute of every day and night.

Berdie and I spent most of time on deck taking in the fresh air. It helped to ward off seasickness. Other guys and gals did the same. The nights were not quiet and the days were full of flirting, talking, and telling jokes with the GI's. The sailors had work to do so we didn't see much of them.

"The sky is beautiful out here, isn't it?" Berdie said, looking up into the cloudless black night. The stars stood out like ice crystals against the backdrop of the rest of the universe. I could see the Milky Way more clearly than I had ever seen. I mused how impossible it seemed that we were heading into a war.

"Yes, it is hard to believe this may be the last time we see anything without the smoke of bombs and other munitions," Letty McMahon, another cabin mate, said.

"Oh my God, Letty, why ever did you agree to become an agent?" Berdie moaned. "You did volunteer, didn't you? We were enjoying the ride on this beautiful ocean liner and you had to go and say that. Did you think we forgot?"

"Beautiful, yeah, right. Sitting huddled out here in army-issued coats and boots with blankets wrapped around our shoulders. Waiting in line a few hours for food, standing while we eat at a 700-foot long, chest high table and then waiting for the next food line to form. Nice vacation." Pest or pessimist described Letty to the T's in her name. I alternated between the two when I wrote about her in my diary. She was definitely the most unhappy person of the lot of us.

"I did volunteer under pretty uncertain circumstances. I was really talked into it by some Brit I thought was cute," Letty told us.

Some Brit? My ears perked up. "What was his

name?" I asked with bile rising in my throat and up into my nose. My palms sweated. Fear of the answer gripped my chest.

"Charles Stanhope. He was quite a talker. One night I was talking to him in a bar in Brooklyn and the next thing I knew I was in Maryland at a training camp. I can't remember what happened in-between those two things. Time went so fast."

"Really, Charles Stanhope?" I saw Charles's neck under my hands choking the life out of him and he was smiling, saying, "Love, I swear you are the only one. You brought me to my knees." I let him go, grabbing his ID and passport and destroyed them with a burning cigarette under my heel. Jerk.

"I guess he slept with you before you left for Maryland?" I asked. Never mind. Don't want to hear it. Wait. Do want to hear it. Did want to know. Didn't want to know. Oh my God, a tennis ball in play. Did she bring him to his knees, too?

"Hey, what kind of girl do you think I am anyway?' She stood and rushed to me and stood close enough I could smell the whiskey on her breath.

"Nooo," she slurred as she almost lost her sea legs, "I most certainly did not, and what business is it of yours if I did?"

"None really. Sorry."

"Ah, you must be sweet on the Brit. Right? Am I right? Am I?"

"No, definitely not." How could I admit anything? I didn't even know for sure. All I knew was if anyone even mentioned being close with Charles, I burned with jealousy mixed with denial, turning my blood green.

"Berdie, come walk with me."

"Sure, I need a break," she said, throwing eye darts at Letty.

We swayed once and then crashed against the rail. The sea had begun to roll, Dark clouds covered the stars and the wind blew my hair in front of my face.

"We'd better go inside. It feels ominous out here," I said.

"Yes, I think so," Berdie said. "Did Letty upset you?"

"Upset me? No." What a lie. "Why?" My hands fisted tight inside my pockets.

"You don't look so good." She rubbed her arms and looked around. "Want to go inside?"

"Must be the waves." I said, "Seventeen days out here is too much for my stomach and my nerves. I thought the ocean trip was to be only fifteen days." I lied. She wouldn't understand about the tornado right behind my eyes.

I followed Berdie through the hatches, corridors, and catwalks to our compartment. When I opened the door, everything in my view spun and I fainted flat out hitting my cheek and chest on the metal trunk we used as a table.

"Hey cutie, nice bed, but it's moving and it's not mine. Where am I, sailor?" I asked through the cotton ball in my mouth.

The cutest teenager taking my pulse said, "Try not to talk, ma'am. Y'all have a fat lip and y'all in sick bay, ma'am." His southern drawl was gentle and comforting.

"You're really cute. Hmm…love…dimple…why here?…have baby or something," I teased, "…you…father…my mouth?"

"No, ma'am, no baby, but I could be the father if you wanted to do the naughty things."

I tried to lift my head to sit up, "Just kidding, ma'am," he blushed. "Try to stay still till I finish taking your pulse. You have some cramping from being seasick and you fainted last night."

"So, why…bed moving…now?"

"Cut swollen lip. You must have bit into it when you hit the floor." He smiled, "Don't worry. It'll feel better little by little as the swelling goes down. Yeah and your eye will open too."

"Seri…ous…ly?"

"I'm serious, ma'am. Doc said you'll be as good as new to kiss your boyfriend at the dock." He smiled and his dimple went deeper.

"So why does the bed feel like it's moving more than normal?" I said squeezing the sheets in my fists as if they were going to save me from falling overboard.

"We're in the middle of a storm right now, Ma'am. Probably for the next two hours, they say."

"Oops, need bucket," I moaned as the ship heaved from side to side for what seemed like forever and I just hung my aching head over the side of the bed and heaved along with it. Seasickness plagued me the rest of the day.

I remembered I'd hit the trunk when I fainted and I had black and blue marks on one breast to

prove it. I felt too sick to eat even after the storm.
Actually no one ate much. I heard a lot of food went
overboard for the fish. Little did we know this food
would be the best many of us would see for the next
three years.

Two days later we could see land and it wasn't
long before the tugboats pulled us to the pier in
Liverpool, England. The sun tried to shine through
the smoke from the three ships docked alongside
ours. This port was as busy as New York. Soldiers,
sailors and airmen saying good-bye to their loved
ones. Tears mingled with smiles of encouragement.

"Look, Berdie, those troops down there are
probably headed for Italy with me. Look at how
they're dressed, pith helmets and all. Maybe I'll be
going with them…" I rambled on as we walked
down the gangplank carrying our duffels, helmets
and radio transmitters.

"I'm going to Paris by plane in the morning. I
wonder what happened to Rick? Anyway, when will
you be leaving?"

"I don't know yet. Someone should meet me
here," I answered and despite my mixed feelings of
jealousy, I hoped it would be Charles. He had flown
to England before I left.

Berdie and I walked along the pier towards the
area where we were to meet the agents to take us on
the next leg of our journey. We stopped before the
gate and turned to each other.

"Berdie, good-bye. God bless you. Remember, I

will see you at the Plaza Hotel in New York City the first of July of 1950. Promise me? This will surely be over a long time before then."

"Yes, the Plaza Hotel, New York City. Bye, Marie. God speed. I will always be your best friend." She gave me a hug. "You have my postal address, right? Maybe something will get to me."

"I do. Be careful, girlfriend." I kissed her cheek and winced as I watched my friend leave to meet a woman who waved a sign with Berdie's code name.

I combed the crowd for someone to signal me, but didn't see anyone. I did find an empty bench along a wall and sat watching the crowds stream on and off the gangplanks. Soldiers, nurses, and crew members came and went. A waiting crowd greeted some. Others went on their way alone, but every person on pier had a purpose and a destination. I wondered about my own destiny and who would greet me.

After two hours still no one came to claim me. I needed a stiff upper lip to get through a feeling of abandonment on a pier in a foreign country. The fear that overtook me after my mother died rose to the surface with a sinister smile, jeering at my resolve. I said a prayer to the Holy Spirit to give me courage. My knees shook as the sun marched toward the horizon but in a moment, my resolve outdid my fear. I was committed to do whatever asked to conquer the malignant forces threatening the world, even if that meant sitting on this bench until morning.

The wooden bench became a planning station for what I would do next if no one came for me. I could stay where I was, but not for long without shelter and food. I could walk through the gate leading outside the fence to the enclosed area where it might be easier for my contact to find me. I could pass through immigration. I had my passport. I could take a cab to a hotel, secure a room, and think. I could go to the United States Embassy in London tomorrow. My mind revolved in circles until I saw a cute tall blond guy with wire-rimmed glass and a baggy raincoat walking toward me. Thank God. I was out of ideas and would soon have to make a decision. Cad, scallywag, scoundrel, two-timer, rogue. But my heart still prayed he might be an angel.

"Charles Stanhope here, love, at your service." His big beautiful smile and twinkling blue eyes melted all those ugly thoughts.

I stood and he took hold of my arms and pulled me close to his face. I inhaled his beautiful fragrance before letting out a giant sigh of relief. He kissed me first on my cheek then on my still swollen lip and sore purple eye. My heart whirled like a carousel as I relaxed into his arms and my helmet clanged to the ground when I reached around his neck. Was I in love with his man or just relieved to see a familiar face? I was sure I wasn't in love. Maybe lust would be the word.

"You look wonderful, love, but what's this? A black eye? Bad cat fight at sea?"

I scowled. "I bet you'd like that…the dream of many men? Met lots of handsome soldiers. Bertie from my Italian class and I became cabin mates with four other women. We played a lot of gin rummy and Scrabble. No cat fight, at least not physical. I fainted just as a storm hit the ship and I hit a trunk on the way to the floor, nothing serious."

"Well, lucky it was not a storm of bombs. German aircraft have been right lively lately."

"The destroyers that came along with us did a fair amount of firing at two or three fighter planes one night."

He pulled me close again and whispered in my ear. "Come. We have a room waiting. It's more than two hundred miles to London so we shall stop for dinner and the night. Martin waits for us in the car park."

No one other than I would have thought of Charles Stanhope as a Romeo, but he had my heart, colorful eye, swollen lip and all. I enjoyed the Charles I remembered for a few minutes.

Soon enough the worm of suspicion crawled out, "How do you know I want to go with you to a room reserved for us? We have to have a talk."

"Certainly. What about? We can discuss anything or anyone you like. Come on. I have something in mind to discuss too, love."

He steered me along with one hand on my elbow and one on my duffel. I carried my helmet and radio. I waited to speak again until I rested in the seat of, what? An Aston Martin, one of the fastest cars on the road.

"Here, love. Place your things in the boot."

"What?"

"The boot, you know. Ah yes, for Americans…the trunk."

"Oh, I remember that from MacPherson. I guess I have to learn a new language here."

"Almost, but not totally." He closed the boot. I sat in the passenger seat on the left side of the car. He put the car in gear and we were off in a whirlwind. No holding this man back.

"Do you like the speed?" he said over the roar of the engine.

"Yes, I love it."

ℭHAPTER TWELVE

THE ASTON MARTIN WAS SUPERB, I was fortunate to still have had it after losing most other things our father had acquired over the years. With Marie at my side, I was the richest man in the world. She belonged with me here in this car, at this time, in this country, on this day.

The motorway was devoid of traffic and I had enough petrol for the trip. Chuffy, that's it, I felt chuffy, happy and the effects of the war dissolved with each kilometer.

"So, England, before it bursts into the beauty of spring, is before your eyes," I said, "What do you think?"

"Beautiful, just colder than I thought."

"Are you cold, love? There is a rug behind you. The heater in this old buggy does not function very well at the moment. Sorry."

"Hmm, nice." She wrapped half the blanket around her legs that I adored, hiked the rest up to her chin that I loved to kiss and closed her eyes.

Soon I heard tiny bubbles of a snore. Poor darling. She looked exhausted and frail with that purple eye. All I wanted to do was to hold her in my arms.

After an hour or so, she stirred. I reached under the rug for her hand, but found her knee. She did not move my hand away. Her eyes were still closed and the sun shone on her face as we cruised along.

Finally she shifted and turned to look at me, but did not speak. She set me full of questions. Had she lost interest in me? Had I not shown enough interest in her the last time we met? She questioned my faithfulness. That was it. Later, I learned I was right on that score. She did question my faithfulness. That was something we had to set right.

"What is it, Marie? What would you like to discuss, love?"

"Okay." She yawned before saying, "I think we should discuss relationships. Ours, for one, and ours with others, for another. There, just two items for discussion."

"Marie, you are quite bold for a woman your age. Most American women do not talk about intimate relationships."

"Am I bold? Well, I like to be honest," she answered folding her lips inward and her hands in her lap. "What do you know about what most American women talk about? I thought I heard you say I was the only one?"

She turned to face me, turned out her lower lip and wrinkled her brow. Then of course I had to smile at her girlish pout. "What has brought this on? Marie, have you found another bloke to love?"

"Me? Nooo. I thought you might have intimate

moments apart from me. After all, before you came to Mario's, I hadn't heard from you in over a year."

"Me?" I chuckled. "Do you mean ladies I have spent time with since I met you?"

"Yes, exactly. Have you er…er…slept with anyone else?"

"Listen, darling, you are the only one for me. I have no others, nor have I been with any other since I met you. Believe me, love, I would not play that game with you."

"Oh, really?" she purred.

"What can I do to rid you of these noxious thoughts?" I squinted at an oncoming truck speeding towards us and swerving from his lane into ours.

"I'll think of something, just give me some time," she said. "I promise it won't hurt. I'll be gentle," she giggled.

Just then a front tire blew out and we swerved off the road into a meadow as the truck passed us. I thought I saw the muzzle of a gun out his side window, but did not speak of it. I did not want to unnerve Marie.

"Oh, my goodness, Charles, That truck? Did he purposely push us off the road?"

"No, I don't think so. He is probably a local farmer." I kept my suspicion of gunfire blowing out the tire to myself. In some circles, my undercover work was not laudable.

"It is nothing…really. No need to fret, love. I'll change the tire. Be done in a few."

Marie stepped out of the car and gazed at the countryside. She crossed her arms and faced the western sun. The breeze blew her hair back and she radiated timeless beauty. Her eyes sparkled and her cheeks glowed. The little sleep she had in the car had done her well.

Soon, we were back on the road.

"Yes, Mr. Stanhope, I think I shall. Your tire changing skill has convinced me I should take advantage of you. Yes, indeed, one room."

Then she changed her mind.

"Wait," she interrupted herself. "Maybe I want my own room. I have to think about this. After all, we have not talked to each other in days."

"No, love, please no." I moaned, "I have been waiting for you in the dark of my single bed for more than twenty-nine days. Have pity on a poor Englishman."

"Ah, poor fellow," she said. "Will we be in London before noon tomorrow?"

"No changing subjects," I declared as we entered the car park. She did not say another word. Nothing more. "Yes, if you insist, love, we will. Unless we stay in bed all night and all morning. But to be honest, I just left Major Johnson. He will be in and he is the man to see tomorrow," I said.

"I do insist. Thank you very much."

"Off we go, then. London first thing in the morning. Dinner and bed now. One room or two? I insist on one."

"Lucky me," she said. "I will share with you, Stanhope...I think."

I threw my hands in the air. "One room, love. You are coming with me." I put my arm around her shoulder where it should have been all day and marched her into the lodging.

What was it I wanted from Marie? What did she want from me? Would she have me as her husband or was she timid about a permanent relationship with a spy who would be leaving her alone and often.

Just who in god's name was I? I didn't recognize myself. This yearning I had for something permanent with her was new to me. The war, with its danger of death so close, had changed me. There may not be a future for finding love a comfort and priority. Some found love whenever and wherever they could with whomever they met on the spur of the moment, just for the moment. Not for me, I wanted Marie forever. I adored her. Would she marry me? Should I ask her tonight? No, tomorrow, after she had her orders to stay in England.

We spent the night together in the same room in the same bed. Marie charmed me. She was a soft kitten at one time and a tiger the next. I could not get enough of her.

The next day Charles and I arrived in London. The mist and fog covered much of the devastation that Hitler's blitz had caused. The bombs had hit many of the train stations destroying the lines they served. The remaining ones provided shelter when the air raid sirens sounded. Marie would learn soon enough where to go until the all-clear sounded.

We stood in front of a three-story brick building. The windows were dark. White carved woodwork framed the door with an elaborate cornice. Inside a darkened green hallway greeted us. The air was as damp and cold inside as out. It seeped deep through my clothes into my bones. My skin crawled with goose bumps. So this was London, fog, mist and more fog.

"Most of our offices are situated around this square. You will learn soon which offices are in which buildings. Your living quarters are over in the Mayfair district, walking distance from here. Quite safe." Charles said.

"Wait, What are you saying. I thought I was going to Italy. What's happened? Why do I need living quarters here?"

"I have been reluctant to tell you. I think you will be here for a time. We will find out in a minute."

"Good, then let's go up. I'm ready," she said with a nervous grin. "Wait, I'm not ready." She took out her compact and checked her eye, touching it with a puff of powder then applied fresh lipstick. "Okay, now I'm ready."

"Beautiful." He lifted my chin and stole a kiss.

"Charles," I said, "you give me chills. How you seduce me with just a touch eludes comprehension."

At a third floor window I moved the black curtain aside and sighed as I saw the devastation the German Blitzkrieg had rained on London. Walls without roofs stood around nothing but debris, windows were missing in others, piles of rubble slopped to caverns that used to be streets. Like a cold electric shock, the seriousness of my new work came to the forefront again. I would do anything I was asked including staying in London.

Major Johnson's office was small, but it had everything it needed, from a large mahogany desk, three file cabinets, and a smaller desk with a typewriter, a two-way radio, and a big green glass ashtray filled with cigar stubs. The boarded window above a yellow settee shut out daylight. Two overhead lights took the place of the blackened skylight. The nameplate on the desk read, Major Peter Johnson.

Major Johnson relaxed with his chair tilted back and feet on the desk. He looked up from some papers he was reading. "Oh, Charles, I did not expect you back. You must be Marie Gentile." He came around the desk, put his cigar in the ashtray and offered me his huge hand. "Major Peter Johnson." His chocolate eyes twinkled. His smile widened up to his gray temples. He stood over six feet, broad-shouldered and slim-waisted. He looked fit and healthy.

"Stanhope, be a gentleman, help the lady off with her coat. You're welcome to stay, too. Sit. Please. Guess you two have plans for tonight so I won't be long," Major Johnson pointed to the two chairs in front of his desk.

"Thank you, sir." Charles helped me out of my coat. He laid it on the settee and we took our seats in front of the desk.

Major Johnson handed me a clipboard with papers to complete with my vital information. "Fill in all the information. Bring it tomorrow afternoon. It is redundant, I know. You probably filled something like this out at least a hundred times, but we need this one for our files here."

He continued. "Just so you know exactly what you are getting into, the last pages are a copy of Ernie Pile's newspaper reports. Read them and look around you tomorrow morning on your walk here. Those reports and what you observe will give you a feel for what the people here have suffered."

"Yes, sir. Charles says I'll stay in the Mayfair district. May I ask how long, sir, before I go to Africa or Italy?"

He ignored my question, "It's a small flat you'll share with another woman. You'll have to do your own housekeeping and cooking." He opened his desk drawer. "Here's a ration book for food and a key to the flat. You will get another book as soon as we get them."

"Thank you, sir." I put the book of coupons and key in my purse. I looked at Charles but he had nothing to say.

"Tomorrow Charles will come for you and bring you to the office downstairs to meet your co-workers. The chaps there will fill you in on what you have to do. Mostly working together to decode messages."

"Downstairs, sir?"

"Yes, the leaflets you wrote with Charles were excellent, so part of your assignment is to create "black" propaganda that we will pass on to the enemy soldiers. Hopefully what you write will break their morale and send them packing. Basically lies…seems an effective tool so far. You will disguise the truth and develop rumors. Also, of course, you'll code messages."

"Not only disheartening rumors, but encouraging ones to the resisters," Charles added.

"I'm ready, sir, but what about Africa and Italy?" Persistence did not escape me today.

"Good girl. Oh, Italy. Yes, No. You'll be staying with us. Doesn't look like Italy is in the picture for you," he said abruptly without explanation.

As we left Major Johnson's office, an ear-piercing siren made me jump. The Major and Charles rushed me down the stairs into the dark musty basement serving as a bomb shelter. I would learn the locations of other shelters between here and my apartment before the end of the week.

A shrill buzz pierced my ears. "What's that?" I asked covering my ears as I huddled between the Major and Charles on the floor.

"Bombs from across the channel."

"Headed for us?" I began to quake. My teeth chattered. Charles put his arm around my shoulders. I looked around. About one hundred other people came into the shelter from the building and the street. They looked so calm compared to me.

"We will not know until it hits, love. Think about something else. Think about how much I care

about you, how sweet I think you are, how I
tantalize you with my wit and courage and how I
have thought about you every single day since I
stepped into the diner." He kissed me first on the
forehead then on the lips. I longed for more.

I looked around again. People were greeting each
other. Some were laughing. A young girl came
prepared with a huge pot of soup. Was that skimpy
fire supposed to heat the big pot? I was getting an
education.

I cuddled closer to Charles and fell asleep. I
dreamed about black holes in the earth with red and
blue flames reaching to the sky. I awakened with a
start when the all-clear sounded. Most people stood
to leave, but some stayed where they were.

"Why are they staying?" I asked.

"They may not have a place to go. This may be
home for them." My heart wrenched with sadness. I
clutched my parched throat. No words describe
what I thought and felt.

Then Charles quietly said, "But love, just think
you are going to a hotel, eat and then a luxurious
bath. Come."

Major Johnson was in front of us. He turned
around to face us, "Good night, see you in the
morning upstairs, Marie; may I call you Marie? I've
thought it over. Come to my office first. I'll bring
you downstairs."

"Of course, sir," I answered.

"Here is the address of your flat and the name of
your mate." He hid behind the nervousness I saw in
his eyes. Did he never get used to bombs and
shelters and what else I could not even imagine?

We reached the outside and he lit his cigar and went on his way.

There was no getting away from the smell of smoke, children crying, and people rushing every which way with handkerchiefs or scarves covering their noses and mouths. Some wore gas masks. I quickly turned my collar to cover my face except for my eyes, but I wish I could have covered them too because they were stinging from the fumes and because I did not want to view the damage.

CHAPTER THIRTEEN

CHARLES AND I ARRIVED AT the hotel just before a beautiful golden ruby sunset folded under the night sky and curfew. Not one street light lit the way and there were no lights from the pubs on the lower levels. Total darkness loomed around us like a shroud. This was my new life.

Our room was a simple bedroom decorated with faded pink flowered chintz drapes and a pink chenille bedspread. A navy blue frieze wingback chair sat in the corner next to a dark wooden wardrobe and a hotplate sat on a marble-top table on the other side of the wardrobe.

"Oh," I said. "This is lovely. Beats a hammock hanging from a pipe."

Charles opened the door to the bathroom. "Madam, for your pleasure," he said pointing to the white porcelain tub sitting next to the hot water heater. "One little match to warm you," he said and lit the fire ring under the tank. "Ready in an hour or two."

"Lovely," I said, "really, Charles." I had lost my smartass attitude. My brain had slowed. I had so much to digest in this new world and felt tongue-tied. The interview with the Major, the shelter, the hotel, the room and even the bed looked like pages in a book. I felt like I was drifting on the ocean again. I had to look at Charles, to find his familiar face and eyes and anchor myself.

Charles looked perplexed, "Love, what is it?" he said, "Something wrong?"

"Huh?" He put his arms around me and I looked into his beautiful blue eyes. "So many new things in such a short time. I thought I knew how it would be for me, but the streets, the people, you, the Major, bombs, everything startles me, makes me shiver and shake."

"I can take care of that for you." He gave me as wicked a smile as any Svengali could, but he was too sweet by far to be wicked. "Come here, love." He had shed his outerwear and was completely at ease with the sleeves of his shirt rolled up.

"No, not yet. Questions first, remember?" Energy had built into my voice. I had come back to the real world.

"Right."

"Charles?"

"What?"

"I'm starving," I blurted out."

"I have ordered some food." He walked to the wardrobe and brought out a bottle of sherry. I went to the bathroom for two glasses I had seen there. He opened the bottle and poured the beautiful amber liquid.

I inhaled from the top of my glass and sipped the sweetness holding it a few second on the roof of my mouth.

"Beautiful, Charles. Thank you. I hadn't realized how much I missed on that ship." I relaxed into the wingback and studied him for a moment. His eyes darkened under my scrutiny. He waited for me to speak.

"So," I began, "I met a woman who says you recruited her in Brooklyn?" I waited for him to respond. I wanted to hear an answer, yet I didn't want an answer. What the hell did I want? We hadn't made any promises about courtship or dating or seeing other people. But the thought of Charles with other women niggled at me.

"Well, yes, I suppose." Now, he waited. "Marie, what else are you asking me?"

"I have to be frank. There's no other way. Did you sleep with her, too?" I spit out the question with a bit of yellow venom.

"Noooo, I don't think so and if I did, it was before I met you. I have not gone with anyone since I left you on the train. I told you. Why do you persist? Are you looking for an excuse to leave? You know you do not need one. I will take you to your flat. We can do that!" Lines creased his brow. He passed his hand through his hair and rubbed the back of his neck.

I looked into those gorgeous blue eyes. "I do have one more question. Why am I not on my way to Italy? You seem to know the Major well. Do you know why I've been detained here?"

"You were on your way as far as I knew a short

while ago, but the commander wanted you here. I am not privileged to know his reasons. I could guess it was because the leaflets we submitted were good for the morale of the resistance in Sicily. So, as the Major said you will be doing the same work here…and one other thing," he hesitated there.

"And what might that be?" I asked, but he wasn't forthcoming. "Charles, tell me. Was it because they think I'm not ready?"

"No, not at all."

"Well, why are you hesitating?"

"Well, yes, in a way."

"Well, yourself, Charles, What is it? Is it a secret mission? I want to know. I should know. Don't you think I should know?" My temper was getting the best of me slowly but surely.

I was not used to being last to know. In Mario's office I was the first to know most things. After all, I was his right hand and his sister.

"In a way, very dangerous if I tell you," he slowed his speech.

"Dangerous for you? I don't understand." Not only frustrated but damn angry, I took a cigarette out of my purse. When Charles lit it for me, I looked up at him through the smoke. His eyelids were heavy. He sat down on the edge of the bed.

"I asked," he whispered. I thought I had heard him wrong.

"What? I can't hear you."

His face paled and he said, "I asked for you."

"And why would you do that? I didn't think you worked for the Major."

"I don't work *for* him. I work *with* him and I am

sorry. I was selfish. I wanted you close to me."

"And you thought to ask without telling me first." I crushed my cigarette in the ashtray, walked into the bathroom and slammed the door. *The nerve of him. How dare he. He knows me better than that. Doesn't he?* I paced back and forth alongside the tub. That was not helping me. I twisted my hands together. I looked in the mirror and began to smile… *I think he does know me better than I know myself. I was glad he wanted me close. How could I not be? I was smitten by this fellow, Charles Stanhope, from our first meeting at the diner.*

I went back into the bedroom and walked over to stand directly in front of him where he still sat on the edge of the bed, "How close?

"What?"

"How close did you want me? Do you mean this close?" I stood about three feet away.

"No,"

"How about this?" I took a step towards him.

"No, Marie," he grabbed my arms and pulled me to him and we rolled onto the bed laughing.

"Thank you, Mr. Stanhope, I certainly appreciate you asking." We were lying side by side facing each other. "But why?"

"I am in love with you, Marie. I knew it in America and I know it now. I want to be with you." He touched my face pushing my hair back behind my ear. The simplicity of his confession reached into the well where I hid my emotions. My tears rolled onto the pillow and Charles kissed my sore eye.

"Ah ha, now the truth comes out, you just want

my body," I whispered. His lips covered my mouth. My hands touched his face to encourage him further. His hands found their way under my blouse along my spine sending heat to every cell in my body. He caressed my waist, my hips, back up to my shoulder, planting kisses from my ear down my arm to my palm. First my left arm, then my right, then to my throat, chin and lips again. His tongue slipped across my lower lip.

"And you, Marie. Do you love me?" His tongue slid along my lip again and stopped waiting for a response. I pulled my head away when someone knocked on the door.

"I don't know, but I love doing this with you," I whispered and reached up to wrap my arms around his neck and rubbed my cheeks on his five o'clock shadow.

"And I like what you're doing."

I liked Charles more than I wanted to admit and I was drowning in his tenderness. Happy little nerves tingled in my arms as I held them around him. Euphoria invaded me. I loved being with him again, but I was not up to admitting love if that was what he wanted to hear. I really didn't know.

Another knock.

"That will do for now," he said in a warm accepting voice and went to the door. It was our dinner. We ate roast beef sandwiches in bed and stayed all night in each other's arms not wishing to see the light of dawn. In the morning I washed in a bath of lavender luxurious bubbles and hot water and then left the magic for reality.

Grosvenor's Square was not far from the hotel, so we took advantage of the morning air and walked to the office. It was the end of winter and the fragrance of new grass and buds on the trees invigorated me. I turned to Charles, "This is a beautiful place, Charles. Is your office near here?"

"I don't have an office. Marie, I cannot tell you anything about where I go or what I do. Suffice to know sometimes I am close by and sometimes in another country, but not in America anymore."

"You make me nervous. Will you be close today and will we meet later?"

"I can't say. When you are done at work, go to your flat, meet your flat mate, have dinner and a quiet evening. I don't know when I will see you again. I shall try to get word to you or come, but I do not think it will be this evening.

"Remember I told you about the Townhouse I own with my brothers and sister. Basically, that is Charles Stanhope's address. However, I do not stay there much. I travel most of the time, you know that, too. I can't tell you where exactly. You cannot go wherever I go, and if you did, let's just say this, love, it would be very dangerous, deadly dangerous."

My heart lost more than a beat. I gasped for air. Charles brought me to him. I said a prayer into his vest, "Oh, my God, wherever you are, always come back."

"Marie, keep walking and don't look at me. I

will drop your duffel off at your flat. Darling, remember to find the nearest bomb shelter on these streets and at your flat."

By the time I could respond, he had turned and walked in another direction. This world was certainly an unpredictable place. I looked around to get my bearings and walked directly to the Major's office.

"Good morning," I said to the Major after I knocked and opened the door to the smoke-filled office. He stayed seated leaning on the back legs of his chair, dragging on the god-awful cigar.

"Trust you had a restful evening after your first shelter experience. If anything, you faced it like a brave little soldier," he said as if I were a child. I guess in some ways I was to him. This was totally new to me like going from kindergarten to college in a day. He knew I had never had to hide from bombs.

"Yes, I did. But, how will I be the next time the siren blows? What if I am alone?" I was holding my purse like a shield up to my chest.

"Just follow the crowd to a shelter. All Londoners know where they are. Sad to say, they are experienced."

"Thank you, sir. I don't know how brave I'd have looked without you and Charles beside me. I suppose I will learn to always show some bravado. Do you think so, sir?"

"Yes, I'm sure. Undoubtedly," he smiled, but

then his lips drooped a little at the corners. "Listen, before we go to your office, I want to say something personal. I say this to every American who comes into this office. Men and women. So don't take offense."

"Why would I take offense, sir? I'm a big girl."

"We don't really know the future, do we? Nor do we know how much time we have together."

"No, sir."

"So I am not sure how to say this."

"What sir, do you want me to go back to the U.S.? Is that what you're trying to say?"

"No, no, not at all. That's not it. I don't know why I stumble when I say this and I say it to all new members of my team. Here it is in a nutshell: be careful with your heart, Marie. These are uncertain times. The future is nothing to trifle with, not now anyway. What I mean is, well, just be careful."

"Yes, sir, I understand," I said, looking right at him. He seemed older this morning. I noticed his hair, more gray then I'd noticed yesterday, and he had dark circles under his eyes. I guessed my father would be the Major's age. I imagined my father would have said the same thing to me.

"I'll be careful, sir. Thank you."

"Good. Come on. I'll take you to your office." He put on his Army waist jacket.

I followed him down a flight of stairs and into a small office. Beyond the door sat four desks in the middle of the room facing each other in a square. Each desk had a typewriter and there was some other kind of typewriter on a table in the corner. Two young people came to greet me.

"Hello, I'm Joe Oliver. Nice to meet you." He took hold of my hand with a strong grip. "I'll talk with you more a little later. I have something urgent to do."

"I'm Ethel Rubenstein." The tiny brunette, just about five feet tall, came next with a warm friendly smile. I felt good about both of them.

"I'm your flat mate," said Ethel. "I thought I would see you last night. What happened to you?"

"Uh…oh," Was it forbidden to speak about Charles? I didn't know so I told a white lie. "I stayed with a friend in Liverpool. I hope you didn't worry. Sick from the long days at sea, I just wanted to stay still for a couple of hours. I slept without moving on her sofa until this morning." I thought I felt secretive, like a secret agent.

"Really, I didn't know you knew anyone in England," she said.

I frowned cocking my head to the side and squinting, "Really? What do you know about me?"

"Oh, I don't know why I said that. You're right. I don't know anything about you except that yesterday you were here with Charles Stanhope."

"So much for a secret agent," I said.

Ethel glanced at Joe who was still busy with some paper on his desk.

"We all know Charles and we looked for you. Then we saw you in the shelter with him. Anyway, welcome to this abode. We sometimes think of this as home. Long shifts are not unusual. There is a cot, blankets and a hotplate in the other room over there." She pointed to another door.

I glanced at the Major to say good-bye, but he had already left.

"So, what do you know about me, Ethel? I don't know anything about you."

"What's there to know? I'm from Chicago. I graduated from Chicago Teachers' College. I speak Yiddish and English. Charles thought I'd be good at this. He was right. I can read Hebrew, too, and some messages come that way. So, how 'bout you?"

"Let me hang my coat first. Joe, do you want to hear about me or is it just Ethel?" I answered with a smile, but thought the nerve of her. Who was she? Was she my superior? I didn't know. I thought I'd better be pleasant at the very least. It's normal to act interested in a person you have just met. *Oh, for goodness sakes.* My nerves were overworked. I had better settle down and be friendly.

I walked to the opposite end of the room, hung my coat on the rack in the corner and sat at the empty desk across from Ethel and next to Joe.

"So, you know my name. I'm from New Jersey. I graduated from New Jersey Women's College at Rutgers University. I'm almost 30 years old and already a widow. A plague of this damned war. I worked in my brother's law office before signing up for this."

Joe clapped his hands and jumped up. "I've got it," he said to no one in particular.

"What?" I asked.

"Solved this code," he said and showed me a list of the final notes he'd used to decipher this particular message.

"Good job." I applauded Joe. He went on quickly to continue revealing the entire message that had come from Anzio, Italy.

Ethel continued to probe, "Do you have children?"

"Do you?" I asked with a candied, innocent smile. "Why do you want to know?"

"Don't know. Just curious. I've heard of an agent who left her two children with her mother, thought maybe she was you," Ethel said.

"Me? No, no little ones. No boyfriend. Just me."

She flipped her short bob behind her ear revealing a beautiful oval face and deep brown eyes. "No, none for me either. I'm ready to get to work. Thank you for the interview, Miss Ruben. It was marvelous. We'll talk more tonight. Okay?"

"Yes, I'll walk with you to the flat later. I have some sausage and potatoes for our dinner."

"Thanks. Now, let's get to work. What shall I do first?" I asked and looked at Ethel. "By the way, can I smoke here?" I fished in my purse for my cigarettes. When I looked up, two pairs of eyes above wrinkled noses stared at me. I stopped fishing and sat down.

"Oh, okay, I'll just finish these papers for the Major," I said and got to work.

CHAPTER FOURTEEN

"WELL, THIS IS IT," SAID Ethel, unlocking the door
to the flat. "Behold, our gracious living room comes
first. The chairs are not too bad, but the sofa has a
spring in the middle section that could tear your
spine out if you're not careful. Here, touch it, so
you know where it is." She took my hand. Ethel had
a slight tremor. "I kind of like the wallpaper, don't
you?"

"I love the perfect water stains, like they are
meant to be there, a nice contrast to the white
hydrangeas," I said.

"The kitchen is through those curtains. It's just a
small alcove with a two-burner stove and tiny oven.
Nothing like home, but then nothing in England is
like home. Here's the one bedroom. We have to
share." She opened a door opposite the front door.
"You can take the top two drawers in the bureau
and the right side of the closet."

"I brought a set of sheets and a towel with me."

"Good. We're lucky we have these old

threadbare sheets and blankets. You can save yours if you like. If you have to buy them here, they are very expensive in the stores right now. The bathroom is over there," Ethel pointed to another door off the living room.

"Right and I need to use it immediately, thank you." The wooden tank for the toilet was attached to pipes running up behind the seat and then into and out of the tank near the ceiling and up to the flat above us. A long pull chain released the flusher. A showerhead stuck out of the wall like a hungry bird. There was no sink. We had to use the kitchen to freshen up.

"You brought your own towel. How about hot water?" Ethel said.

"Hot water?"

"Well, smile, that was a joke. However, hot water is scarce. It is turned on at six a.m. and off at three in the afternoon. Your best bet is to take a quick shower in the morning, never at night, unless you're willing to freeze your boobs," she said with a shimmy.

"I think morning is best. Did you have a flat mate before me?" A picture of Ethel and a young man on the nightstand between the beds prompted me to ask.

"No, not recently. You're the first.

"Not to be nosy, but does your boyfriend stay over? I could ask for a different place if you want."

"No. Really, it's all right. He's not in England any more. He wanted to go undercover to France. So that's where he is. I hope," she said with a troubled look in her eye. "Next time I see him will be the last and it won't be here. I found out he's married."

"Oh? Now why would a smart girl like you get involved with a married man?"

"I, er...."

"Oh, please, never mind. I'm being too personal. Don't answer. I noticed you have a radio in the living room. Does it work?"

Ethel did not answer about the boyfriend, but did about the radio as she walked back into the living room. "Yes, it works. We can listen to Voice of America and BBC. The only station you can trust. The others usually spout rumors to the Germans from the Black Morale Operations Center. You know what that is, don't you?" The edge of her voice had porcupine quills. Did she have it in for me, the old boyfriend, or was it the war overwhelming her? I didn't attempt to understand her hot and cold answers.

"Of course, I do," I said. "But I don't have to explain it to you, do I?" I snapped back.

"No, sorry, I'm a little on edge since Brian left."

Ah, ha, I'm right. "So, listen Ethel, time will help. You're young. You'll meet someone perfect for you. Maybe, not soon. Maybe not till this damn war is over, but I'll bet you ten dollars that you'll forget about Brian and meet someone utterly fantastic and single."

"Thanks, Marie," she said and gave me an unexpected hug. Her sudden warmth chased away the chill I'd had from her unpredictable attitude and the damp gray weather outside the living room window.

"Look," I said, "we have each other to lean on, right? It doesn't look like I'm going anywhere soon. We're Americans stranded on an island. What do you say?" I stretched out my right hand. "Come on and no more snappy remarks. Okay? Even though we will try to be as frank as we can without upsetting the other one." We shook hands before a giant hug. "Should I unpack now or help get the dinner ready?"

"You unpack. I'll cook. I don't mind. It gives me something other than work and Brian to think about. Tomorrow I'll show you where to buy groceries. Do you have your rations book?"

I spent the dark hours of night listening for the insidious hum of incoming doodlebugs and tears fell on my pillow. Hearing far off explosions from hell, I thought how each explosion carried away victims who were loved by someone. Each victim had a family. Each victim was a human being lost or broken forever. Where was God when we needed Him? I had no answer, but my fingers touched my rosary and fisted the beads in my hand. I buried it under my pillow until I heard the siren and someone banging on our door and yelling, "Ethel, hurry!"

Ethel jumped up and grabbed me by the arm. "Come on. We have to go. Get your coat and run down to the basement. No lights. Quick," she ordered as if she were the general.

We raced down the steps with the other tenants, an old man and a couple. The man and wife each carried a child. The kids were so used to the racket they were still asleep on their parents' shoulders.

The men and women in our building had dug a passage from the basement to a nearby and new unfinished Tube station that would have been under our street. It provided a great shelter. Some of the best places to find shelter were indeed the Tubes. The corrugated metal on the walls reinforced the concrete, providing additional protection.

"Those two cots are ours," she said. "You can try to sleep. I never do much but doze every so often until morning."

The smell of wet wool, stagnant water, and human perspiration filled every breath I inhaled, but at least we were underground. I didn't feel safe enough to even close my eyes. "Does anyone sleep?" I asked.

Ethel just shrugged her shoulders and pointed to the children.

"What are those things?" I pointed to something that looked like an animal cage.

"Those cages? They are Morrison shelters. They are supposed to withstand the blow-out from bombing," Ethel said. The parents put the kids inside the Morrison on and under thick blue wool blankets.

Before bedding down, Ethel said, "Everyone, this is Marie, my new flat mate."

The parents greeted me with handshakes and friendly smiles. "Wish I could offer you some tea," the wife said. I am Marion Foster and this is Ian, my husband. You must come up to our flat soon for a nice chat. Right now we have to bed down with the children or they are likely to wake.

The elderly gentleman gave a strong healthy handshake. His watery hazel eyes wandered over me like a young man's. "So, I hear you are another Yank from New York? Are you?"

"I live close to New York in New Jersey."

"I was there once. A busy city. Glad to have you Yanks here. Anything you need, just tell me."

"Why, thank you, sir." I said.""Can you be my knight in shining armor?" I said.

"I have been waiting for you to ask. Anything you want. Well, almost anything. A pretty lady like you doesn't have a knight yet?"

"Actually, I'm not sure…"

"Well, happy to be of service." He took my hand and kissed my knuckles. I gave him my handkerchief and he tucked into his collar. "Thank you, fair lady."

Ethel said, "We'll be here until the all-clean sounds. Try to rest at least."

I went to the cot and put my head down, pulling my coat over me. I was happy for the ugly green heavy woolen thing. Ethel pushed her cot up against mine.

"Marie?"

"Huh?"

"Would you hold my hand?" Ethel asked. Her voice quivered and she reached across the empty space between us.

"Sure, sweetie." I stretched my arm through the sleeve of my coat to her cold fragile palm with the tremor. Was it fear or illness causing her to shake? It did not disappear as she settled. Later I learned she'd suffered from the tremors since childhood.

Me? I fell asleep and awakened to see Gus coming over to me. Where had he been? Why was he so late getting here? He was safe. He hadn't died. It was all a mistake. I moved the cover and he lay next to me.

I opened my eyes to the kerosene lamp and Gus disappeared. Would he ever rest in peace? Would I ever forget him? No, I promised him and myself I would not forget, but he must move on and so must I.

"You are in my heart, Gus." I whispered and kissed the crucifix on my rosary.

"Good evening, Lord Stanhope," Lord Sommers said to me as I stood, part of a small gathering in front of the massive stone fireplace with the glass-eyed boar's head staring at us from above the mantel. Thick velvet drapes covered the French doors to the garden and kept out the draft. Opposite the fireplace an old threadbare tapestry covered the wall, hiding a secret door to the vault on the lower level. This was not the first time I'd been invited to a meeting at the manor house about fifty miles from London This was a cell of wealthy German sympathizers who supported Hitler's takeover of England.

"Good evening, delighted to meet you." I shook hands all around. "We are doing some great work together," I said to these men, fathers and their sons who thought the fashionable thing was to sympathize with Germany, thereby ending the war for England. Their wives and daughters were enjoying drinks and dinner in another room of the great house. A sign of days gone by for most Englishmen, but not for the bit of aristocracy gathered here.

One of the older men spoke up. "Our German contact tells us you are in close with the Führer. Is that so?" He chewed on the end of his cigar and drew close to me.

"Yes, I have contacts in Germany who are close to the Führer's inner circle. I advise the high command of the situation here in England." I sipped my Scotch. It warmed me more than the company to say the least.

"I say, jolly good of you to travel with our planes dropping bombs there on German soil every day."

"Yes, sir, quite disarming, but worth the effort, do you not agree?"

"Of course, of course. Someone has to do it."

"To the Führer." Lord Sommers held his glass high and toasted.

"Heil Hitler." Those gathered around the massive stone fireplace raised their glasses before seating themselves in the plush velvet chairs around the carved mahogany table set with fine rosebud china filled with black market food.

Not particularly religious about saying grace before meals, I did say something in my mind in Latin...*have mercy on us.* I took my place among the others at the dining room table and pretended to enjoy the indulgent meal of roasted pork and beef, potatoes, greens, hot gravy and warm bread. The aromas were delicious but the thought of eating this food while most of the city starved turned my stomach, but not to call attention to myself, I took and swallowed what I could.

"It is quite alarming that the Enigma book could have gone missing for forty-eight hours then returned," the Duke said.

"Odd, I must say," another gentleman added.

"What should we make of it?" Lord Sommers proposed with a mouthful of pork. "Harold?"

"Oh, uh, well," the Duke named Harold wiped a drip of gravy from his chin. "Have you questioned the household staff?"

"I beg your pardon. I trust my staff beyond doubt, sir. Mr. and Mrs. Burroughs are beyond reproach and I daresay everyone in this household is. I myself interviewed them."

"Perhaps a spy among the delivery men from town, I venture to say, may have been curious and, uh, borrowed it," I said as I pushed my food around my plate.

"Gentlemen, consider this, a spy among us," Lord Framingham interjected.

"I object. Don't be absurd, Edmond." Lord Sommers did not hesitate to defend the group. "I hand-chose everyone at this table myself. You all are my closest friends."

"Thank you, sir, for you diligence," I said. I picked up my serviette to dry my sweaty palms. "Gentlemen, please, it is of no use to blame each other. We have the book in our hands again, where it will remain under lock and key. Correct, Lord Sommers?"

"Yes, I myself have checked and rechecked the vault locks today. The code book is now safe inside," Sommers said.

I spoke up, "And I have checked the book itself a few hours ago. There are no missing pages. Nothing has been marked. No discernible fingerprints. Of course," I added, "I cannot know with certainty the Enigma book has not been photographed or copied by very careful operators." *Like me and Marie.* "However, I am quite certain I would have found something left by strange hands if anyone other than ourselves, had touched any part of it. I found none."

Harold said, "Then, let us agree and swear not to let this oversight get back to the homeland. We must keep it between us, keep the disappearance secret from the other sympathizer cells and save face for that matter. Maybe even our own necks."

"Yes, the homeland would likely take physical steps to deter us for this unseemly mistake." I nodded along with the others, taking a cigarette from a gold case. I finally relaxed and lit it, adding to the already smoke-filled room and shared another drink, toasting the success of the Nazi bombing on London that night.

"To the demise of the monarchy and the success of the Reich." We held our glasses high. Ironic, I thought, to see the cut crystal reflect the light from the chandelier while London was in darkness.

"Hurrah."

"Here, here."

"I bid you goodnight, gentlemen," I said. "So, sorry to leave you at this early hour, but I must awaken to be on the road before breakfast. Your honorable leader has given me an assignment." I gave a short bow and retreated to my bedchamber.

I lay awake in a four-poster bed draped with heavy silk brocade at each post and stared at the canopy. Here I was in unimaginable comfort while Marie and the rest of London were probably in a cold damp bomb shelter with a Sterno stove and canned rations.

To what end have I brought Marie? Most likely I will not see her beautiful face or feel her silken hair on my shoulder or hear her cheeky banter. I should have had her sent to Washington D.C. What a selfish fool have I, Charles Stanhope, been? I am no better than the men downstairs. I betrayed her confidence in me.

I imagined Marie with my arms around her when we danced at Ziggy's. She had worn a navy dress with a belt and a rhinestone buckle on her tiny waist. I remembered the night we'd stood and looked at the New York skyline across the Hudson River and how I had kissed her sweet lips and felt her warm body press against me.

I fell into a restful sleep without the least worry that any of these bombastic Nazis fools from dinner would learn about me. These men at tonight's gathering were aching to help the enemy. *I would discredit them and arrest them before this war is over.*

The Duke had assigned me to leave the next morning and travel to the surrounding countryside, recruiting support for the forthcoming invasion of Great Britain by Germany. There would be a meeting in each hamlet. I would speak out against the monarchy. It was a dangerous mission. *Who in his right mind supported a German takeover of the British Isles? Most Brits would die protecting their free society, economy, and government. Nevertheless, an astounding number supported getting rid of all of our immigrants, especially Jews. Some even believed that the King of England himself supported Hitler.*

My counter espionage job for MI6 was to feed disinformation to the enemy. I left the manor house carrying leaflets that my countryman would post in every town should the Germans actually land on English soil. The leaflets announced the surrender of Hitler. The intention was to demoralize the German soldiers so they would retreat back to Germany or surrender as prisoners of war. The Duke and his companions were oblivious to my mission for MI6.

CHAPTER FIFTEEN

I SAT ON THE LUMPY wingchair in our living room writing a letter to Charles. I had not seen him in more than a month and my anxiety level without him increased day by day. *Where was he? What was he doing? Was he a prisoner?* Damn, that man haunted me.

I remembered one evening in Joann's basement. He'd touched my shoulder and when I'd turned to see what he wanted, he'd stared at me from behind those wire-rimmed glasses and said, "You are the most beautiful woman I've ever met. Would you allow me to kiss you?"

"What?" The guys where I grew up didn't ask for permission to kiss a girl. They just moved in until you either surrendered or gave them a good shove. Charles was a different kind of man.

"Kiss you. You know when two people put their lips together like this." He bent closer and I moved closer and *Mama Mia!* I was kissing a Brit in Joann's basement. It was not just a friendly kiss either. It was hot and luscious and I'd wanted more, but I turned back to the typewriter and tapped away.

"You, love, taste and smell most delicious, as I knew you would," he said, as he lit a cigarette. "When this war ends, we will do that more often."

Well, where is he now? Here I am in his country, working till all hours with no one but Ethel to comfort me. Boohoo. I was being such a ninny. I knew his work was as important as mine and I knew I would see him again. I prayed I would see him again.

Except, I didn't even know when I would see him. That woman, whoever she was, who had planted seeds of doubt about Charles would just not go away. Was he really a cad, scoundrel, womanizer? How would I ever know for sure? I better just stop thinking about him. He may, after all, turn out to be the jerk I first assumed he was. I should write a letter to Joann and forget about Charles.

The sirens took me out of my thoughts into reality once more. My building companions and I headed for the shelter as fast as we could. Ethel was not with us. She had gone to market after work and hadn't come home yet. Where the heck was she? I hadn't noticed the time before I heard the sirens, but it was past curfew. She would have to spend the night wherever she was, in whatever shelter she could find.

My heart pounded at the thought of losing her in the maelstrom of doodlebugs. I could hear humming overhead towards their targets. Where was that girl? Where was Charles? What was I doing in London? I should be home listening to Benny Goodman and Frank Sinatra in New Jersey instead of lying in this creepy underground cave. Then I looked at my building friends who were carefully putting the kids to bed in the shelter cage. I began to sob quietly into my coat lapel when I felt the old man, Mr. Merkel, put his arm around me. I buried my face in his chest and wept as if I knew for certain tomorrow would not come this time. He patted my back while the hands on my watch turned slowly.

"Let's pretend," he said, "that this is New Year's Eve, the sirens are just noisemaker and tomorrow is what? What shall be tomorrow?"

"Sure, I can play nice," I said and sat up. "Tomorrow will be the first day of my married life with the man of my dreams. I don't have a good picture of any man in mind."

"Really and why is that?" he asked.

"What's the point?" I pouted as I took the cigarette he offered. We sat back against the wall and inhaled deeply. I exhaled a perfect smoke ring above my head. He made a bigger one.

"I can beat that one." I blew out a bigger smoke ring and we both laughed. "Happy New Year, Mr. Merkel," I said. The all-clear sounded. I kissed him on his soft wrinkled cheek. "Thank you, kind sir. You know exactly how to make a foreigner who is both homesick, overworked and a scaredy-cat feel better."

"Sorry to say, I know exactly what it takes to live through a war." Now he sounded disheartened. "Memories, you know. The trenches often come to mind."

"Well, let's pretend it's New Year's Day and plan a special dinner with turkey and all the trimmings."

"No, my dear, we shall have goose and all the trimmings."

"That'll work," I said, and we walked arm-in-arm through the tunnel and back to our apartments.

"Thank you, God," I whispered and crawled into my bed with a new stiff upper lip.

I slept through the rest of the night and awoke to see Ethel was safe and sound in her bed. A wave of relief washed over me. I let her sleep longer and prepared some toast and tea for our breakfast. When she came to the table, I saw the sling.

"Oh my god, Ethel, what happened? Were you caught in the bombing?"

"No, well—kind of. I fell on the way to the shelter. I covered my face with my hands as I went down and dislocated my shoulder. A man carried me to the shelter. I must have fainted because I woke up in the hospital with this. They discharged me to give the bed to someone worse off than I."

"How did you get home? Weren't you frightened to walk the streets alone?"

"Well, the gentleman who helped me up came to the hospital and made sure I came back here in one piece. We were lucky enough to find a horse-drawn carriage. Came here first and then he went on," she said with a smile on her face.

"Was he charming and handsome?"

"Yes, I think so."

"Oo-la-la! And are you going to see him again?"

"I would like to," she answered me with disappointment in her eyes.

"And him?" I asked and stood to clean the two dishes and cups we had used.

"He said he had a lady."

"Are you coming to work? I know you can't type, but there's a lot to do."

"Yes, if you help me wash and change these clothes," she said.

It was when we were at the sink she mentioned the man's name. "Mr. Stanhope said he had a lady, but his cousin, Charles MacPherson was free. He would tell MacPherson, to call on me if I were interested. I said sure."

I dropped the facecloth in the basin and smiled. *So he is still alive. Why didn't he come in to see me? He knew where I was living. What a fool I've been, thinking again I had a future with Charles Stanhope because he wanted me for a night—no, two nights—in the sack. Who's the jerk? Ole Charlie boy? I don't think so. It's me. I'm the jerk. Well, maybe not jerk. Just a lady in mourning with a vulnerable heart. Holy Mother Mary help me, stiff upper lip and all. What the hell am I thinking? Anything to sabotage the relationship. Right? Hold on there, Marie girl. Nothing is lost. Keep your head on your shoulders and your heart where you want it, with Charles.*

CHAPTER SIXTEEN

May, 1944

THE GRASS IN GROSVENOR SQUARE softened, turned
green and the leaf buds opened. The sun was higher
in the sky, days were longer and nights were
shorter. If the war had been over, May and June of
1944 would have been lovely. Sunshine followed
me home.

With the German retreat from Anzio and the
Normandy coast, life looked better and the end of
the war was in sight. Only a matter of time lay
ahead before Hitler surrendered. Rumors had it he
had indeed left Germany, but we could not verify it.
A countryman said he had seen Hitler get into a
helicopter and head towards Switzerland.

Charles didn't share much even though he would
still disappear for weeks at a time. When he was
gone, I ached to know he was safe. I was always
surprised when I saw him. I never really knew when

he would show up. I could only remember how I felt when I was with him.

Sometimes I would see him coming across the square or hear him outside the office door. It was always him. No illusions as when I used to see Gus.

One Sunday afternoon a knock disturbed my afternoon nap. I jumped out of my dream of Charles and into his arms at the front door. I pulled him inside and closed the door. He kissed me with a hunger I had not felt until then.

"Where is Ethel?" With that, he moved me backwards into the bedroom and turned the lock on the door behind him.

"She's…with MacPherson. At your…townhouse I suppose," I said between kissing him and unbuttoning his shirt. "Charles, I was so worried about you. I thought you might have been uncovered and on a train to Bukenwald. I've missed you too."

"So we are…alone for the day?" he asked between kisses and pulling my sweater up over my head.

"Yes,"

"Good, I need you, love," he whispered full of energy, full of excitement, full of sex.

He nudged me onto the bed, just where I wanted to be, surrounded by him for as long as he wanted.

"I'm hungry," he said about two hours later. "Let's go. I know the perfect place, but you must act like my Italian lover, who favors the Germans."

"Oh, I can do that. *Amore, you are-a so charming and-a handsom-a. Here. I help you relax, Yes?*" I slinked towards him on the bed dressed in my slip.

"Stop right there," he teased, "or you will have to come back to bed and you will never eat dinner."

"Such a spoilsport, Charles. Come on. Let's go." I pulled my blue print dress, the only dress I had, over my head. He kept watching me as I put on my ankle socks and black pumps. Silk stockings had disappeared from the stores months ago. We had to wait for the next troop ship from the States to arrive. The GI's always brought stockings for the ladies in England.

"Lord, I do love you, Marie."

The perfect place was a tiny restaurant hidden in the rubble of London's East Side. La Stella d' Oro had four tables, each covered with a stained white cloth, and an empty bottle of Chianti with a melted pink candle. From the kitchen, the aroma of Italian food filled the dining room.

"Charles this-a iz a nice-a place." He turned and leaned in, nuzzled my ear and said, "Love, you are fabulous. Be careful. German sympathizers often come here. They might know me and must not think I am conspiring with an American."

"Grazie."

"Gino," Charles called out to the cook, who came from the kitchen. "Gino, this is my friend, Margarita, from Palermo."

"*Piacere, signorina.* A pleasure." Charles had told me that Gino pretended not to understand much English, but he often gathered valuable information from the German sympathizers who frequented his restaurant.

"*Anche io,*" I said and turned to Charles, giving him a ferocious kiss on his neck and then his lips. We were in overdrive from an afternoon in bed. I didn't have to pretend to be a lover, only a native Italian. Easy as pie.

"Gino has the best connections for black market foods, so, tonight we dine, not just eat," Charles said as we followed Gino to our table. There were no other diners.

"*Amore*, (love), such a fine quiet place. How did you ever find it?" I hugged his arm and rubbed it while I blew a kiss up to his cheek

"My brother found it before the blitz and we come now and then," Charles answered and looked at the door as an odd couple walked in. One wore a horizontal striped shirt, a blue neckerchief and a beret. The other wore a gray-striped double-breasted suit. Two men.

"If-a only for you English friends that they will-a, hmm…, how do you say, oh, I know, surrender, the bombing, they stop. And-a we have-a no mess like outside. Everything nice and clean."

"Yes, you are right, darling. No mess if England surrenders." Charles smiled so his nose crinkled and he had to push up his eyeglasses. We both stared at each other under the pretense.

"And-a the children, they don't have-a to go-a country. Could stay London with mum and da, no?"

"Yes, yes, love, very good," Charles said, playing along with me and nuzzling my neck about my collar.

"So, how's my accent?" I had found his ear with my lips and whispered.

"Lovely, darling," he said as he glanced over my shoulder to see if anyone else had followed the two men. "Love, a lesson, never sit with your back to the door, too dangerous." Always checking for trouble, that was Charles, that was his MO. Nervous chills would roll down my back every time he did that. And today I knew what he meant when I noticed the two men.

The aromas from the kitchen intoxicated me. For a moment, I remembered my uncle and my brother cooking the Sunday gravy in our little kitchen. They always prepared the meal together. Then someone was behind me. Was it Mario? A weakness crept up my legs and arms and a foul wave of homesickness flooded my insides before I saw the table rise to meet my forehead and I slid to the floor.

A few minutes later I saw Mario standing over me. I moved my lips. "Mario, what are you doing here?" But my voice didn't make a sound. He couldn't hear me. He just turned and walked to the door. I shivered when I saw him leave.

"Mario?" I whispered. I felt a hand under my neck and a cold wet cloth to my forehead. "Mario? What's happened?"

Someone I had never seen before said to me, "No, not Mario. Mr. Sheffield, if you don't mind. You fainted, love," Sheffield said. "Too much fun today? Not enough food, I suppose?"

"Where'sa Mario?"

"Mario? I have not the slightest idea who Mario is. I suppose another lover, *signorina*?"

"Yes, I saw-a him. He was-a here."

"Sorry, love," Sheffield said, "You must have been dreaming."

Who was this guy calling me love? He definitely was not Charles and I wanted to spit in his face. The nerve of him calling me love. Should I smack him? I tried to lift my hand, but it was as heavy as a lead cannon ball. Mr. Sheffield walked to the other side of the room.

"Ah, Mr. Stanhope, you're awake. How's your head? Sorry about that bump. You understand. You fell over quickly. Chloroform does that to a person."

I opened my eyes in a darkened room. The only light came from the doorway into the alley where the trash was and a bare incandescent light bulb overhead. I would have stood, but my arms were tied behind my back and my ankles secured to a chair. I would have called to Marie on the cot between stacked boxes of spaghetti and canned tomatoes, but a rag that tasted like cheese cut the corners of my lips and was knotted behind my head.

I did not have my glasses. I could only squint across the room at another person tied to a chair. It looked like Gino, but I wasn't sure. I wanted to close my eyes and sleep. My head hurt. Where was Marie?

Cold water drenched my head and dripped down

my neck. It did help alert my senses to the danger. A short muscular thug with dark beady eyes and a swastika tattooed on the back of his hand stared down at me. He spoke Russian. I understood everything, but did not let him know. He wanted to know where the Enigma code book was stored. I shrugged my shoulders and frowned at him.

"What?" I said. "Sorry sir, you will have to please speak English."

Another guy leaned over Marie with a glass of water. He appeared to be a gentleman and a scholar, perhaps a professor.

"Mario?" she whispered. "Mario? What's happened?"

"No, not Mario, Mr. Sheffield if you don't mind—You fainted, love," Sheffield said to her. "Too much fun today? Not enough food, I suppose?"

He coaxed her awake until she was alert enough to sit up and see me. In a thick Italian accent she said, "What have you done to my friend over there?"

"Just a little torture. Nothing to worry about," he answered in English.

She leaned into his face. "Hmm, you smell delicious. Is-a your cologne from Paris?"

"Why yes? Do you like it? I do and I like you."

"I was just there last week, and my German friend-a. He smelled just-a like you. Very masculino, no?" She hummed. "I stand now? Pleeese-a?" she asked. She smiled at him and then pursed her lips.

"Certainly," he said and helped her up. She put

her hands on his chest. "Please, Mr…er, oh, you-a tell me your name again, yes?" She was purring like a cat and moving closer to him.

"Sheffield," he said as he put his arms around her waist.

I wanted to ring his bloody arms out of their sockets. He was such a pig. Touching Marie as if she were his property.

"Well-a, Mr. Sheffield, you like-a the man, Hitler?"

"Of course. He will lead the world soon. Imagine, a man like him creating a clean world with no Jews."

"So, why-a you want-a to hurt us? We are nobody important. You see-a that man over there, that blond with the glasses and blue eyes, he is-a nothing…only a sniveling little boy with glasses. He is not even a man, you know what I mean, no?" she said and rubbed her breasts across his chest. "But you, you look like a real man to me. Oops, I need-a some lipstick, you no mind? I think-a I go to the ladies' room, yes?"

Marie was perfect. She moved seductively and Sheffield, fool that he was, let his guard down. "Yes, I will help you, darling," he said. "I can watch, you know, in case you fall again."

I will use my knife on him, slice him slowly and pull his guts out onto the floor while he watches me smile.

Marie held his arm within hers and in one swift move she shoved her other fist into his Adam's apple, pulled his arm behind his back, and smashed his face into the table in front of me with her whole body on top of his back. She grabbed the gun inside her sweater and put it to his head in another swift move.

The thug scrambled towards her, but he did not make it. Gino tumbled forward in his chair and tripped the man. His head made the sound of a sledgehammer against the concrete floor. Blood poured down his face and blinded him. He lifted his head once and then went unconscious hitting the concrete again.

Marie pushed the muzzle into Sheffield's face and took a breath before she said, "Now, how you-a say, Mister Sheffield…untie my friends, or I shoot you face off."

She let him up with the cold metal of the muzzle pressing on his temple. When Sheffield finished with my ropes, I grabbed him by the throat, threw him down, and hog-tied the traitorous swine. Marie set Gino free. He tied the bloody thug then telephoned the precinct.

I looked into Marie's deep-set eyes, "Love, you are beautiful…and so sexy. Will you marry me?" I played at putting her hair right.

"Are you crazy? What's the point? The world is coming to an end or we will…sooner or later." She laughed, pushed me into the chair, climbed into my lap, and ravished me with kisses.

When she took her mouth away from mine, I shouted, "Gino, bring the spaghetti, we're hungry."

That night I dreamed: I saw myself waking in the

back room of Gino's restaurant. "Mario, what are you doing here?" But my voice didn't make a sound. He couldn't hear me. He just turned and walked to the door. I shivered when I saw him leave. Still dreaming, I heard myself say, "Mario?" I felt a hand under my neck and a cold wet cloth to my forehead. "Mario? What happened?"

"Charles, I am Charles. Marie, listen to me. I am Charles. You fainted, love," he said. "Too much fun today? Not enough food, I suppose?"

"Where's Mario?"

"Mario? Your brother?"

"Yes, I saw him. He was here."

"Love, no, just Gino and I are here, hold my arm. Come. Up you go."

He lifted me to my seat at the table and pulled his chair close to mine. Gino brought me a glass of water.

Charles's voice was as smooth as warm milk and honey on my shattered nerves. I pulled myself together, but grief overtook me. Tears rained on my cheeks. I wiped them with my hands.

"Charles?"

"Yes, love?

"I want to go home, home to the United States of America, home to New Jersey." Tears streamed down my cheeks. "Please, I want to go home. No bombings there, no charades, no looking over shoulders."

I awakened in a pool of perspiration. What was happening? Did my dream show me my true desires, my fears or just a jumble of memories from the day?

The devastation here, the coding and decoding messages of sabotage, troop movements, ammunition sites, and death looming over me day after day had become more than I could handle. There was no relief. Was this feeling what they called battle fatigue or homesickness? Maybe due to the lack of food? Was that why I felt so sick and disheartened? I didn't know. What about fainting on the ship? Maybe my sickness was fear. Fear of death, fear of losing the war, fear of losing Charles—or maybe fear of winning him.

He had changed my life plan so that I would stay here in England instead of going to Italy. Charles had messed up my plans without a second thought to what I wanted. He had changed them without asking. He had delayed my plan for Italy because he wanted me. I had been in England for over two years. I was pretty sure my orders would never change.

In my dream, I faced my fear. I was afraid of life as it revealed its force at Gino's. Spies watching us, following us and sedating us for information. Could I go on under the conditions?

I stirred and looked at Charles sleeping next to me. "Charles, please." I nudged his shoulder. "Charles, listen to me, please."

He turned to face me. "Yes. What is it, love?

"I want to go home."

"Love, we are home. We are here in the flat."

"Not here. Home to the U.S." I snapped like a firecracker. My nerves were wired hot.

"No, you don't want to go now. I have to talk to you."

"Talk to me? How about listening to me, for once?" I got out of bed and grabbed my robe.

"Marie, darling, I always listen to you."

"Oh, really? Never mind. I need a cigarette. I'm sure you can see I am not okay."

"Yes, I think you are just recovering from today's work. It was unexpected, but you did marvelously well." He smiled and winked at me. "You reacted perfectly."

"How can you say that? It was pure instinct on my part. No thought involved. I was on automatic survival mode."

"That is good, Marie. You did well. That is what a good agent does. Acts on instinct in dangerous situations," he said. "Come here, love. Lie down here next to me. I promise I will take you to the States. Tomorrow, we will ask the Major for places on the next air transport."

Oh my goodness. He said yes. I was shocked. This wonderful man was willing to do what I asked. I looked down at him on the bed. My knees went weak and my heart began to sing.

"Thank you. You know, I adore you," I went back to the bed and cuddled up to him.

"I see that bump on your head did some good. But do you know that I had planned a romantic dinner with you? I planned to tell you how much I really love you. I wanted to say how you help me breathe and how you help me live this miserable life. Just being next to you fills me with energy." He turned and leaned above me. "Will you marry me…tomorrow?"

He wants to marry me? Tomorrow? Now, during

the war? What was he thinking? I wanted to go to New Jersey

"What? Marry? Now? Oh, for goodness sakes, No, no. I can't. We're in a war. You're always leaving. I never know if you're coming back. I couldn't stand losing another husband. Let's end the war first."

Oh my god, the war had defined me. For now, for me, war was all there was…and Charles. I adored Charles, but defeating Hitler was my priority. Not a wedding. A cold chill made me shiver. I was not going anywhere.

"I am so sorry Charles. I am not ready. The world is not ready. I can't. Not now. Marriage means a home, a life with a man close by, not a man leading a double life and traveling with the enemy half the time."

Charles furrowed his soft blond eyebrows and stared at me. I couldn't stand watching him, so I pulled on my robe and walked into the living room to find a cigarette.

He came and took hold of my trembling hand and lit the fag for me.

"Thank you," I said, glad that he didn't say any more about marriage. I didn't want to talk. I wanted to be alone in my confusion. At the same time I didn't want him to leave me. What the heck did I really want?

CHAPTER SEVENTEEN

ETHEL WAS READING THE LATEST edition of *The Daily Mail* at the kitchen table when I walked into the flat. She heard me, but didn't look up. "Hmmm, did you know the old lady next door passed away and no one knew for a week. Can you believe that?"

"I guess with the sirens being quiet lately, no one thought to knock on her door. She had nice neighbors, but no one thought to look in on her. Poor lady. No family?" I said.

Ethel kept reading, "And that girl down the street, you know, the young one, had her baby. She had a boy, at home…with a midwife assisting. God sending hope for the future, I suppose."

I took off my shoes and plopped down on the sofa. Ethel looked over at me and jumped from her chair when she saw the black and blue bump on my forehead.

"Oh my goodness, y're hurt. What happened? Let's see."

"I was chloroformed at Sunday lunch with

Charles. Can you believe it? What's wrong with me? I can't even avoid a table on my way to the floor," I was trying for a joke and a laugh, but it wasn't easy. "And I'm sure it looks worse than it feels, too. Pity me? I need some pity right now." I cried and Ethel hugged me.

"Okay, stay here." She got a bed pillow and stuffed it behind me. "I'll make you some tea and toast."

No sooner had I put my head back, I felt a hot flush of tears.

So much had happened in the past few years since I sat at the diner in New Jersey waiting for Joann. Images rose and fell across the pages of my mind. I saw myself meeting Charles for the first time when he invited himself to sit with me and I saw myself chasing him away.

"Ethel, you know one time my friend Joann and I went looking for Charles at his apartment in Brooklyn when he missed our appointment."

"No kidding. Did you find him?"

"Not there." I stopped talking for a moment and imagined Mario coming to my place at midnight and asking for biscotti when he was about to send me off to the war zone.

"Did I ever tell you I met MacPherson on the train to Ontario?"

"No, what was he like?" Ethel asked.

"Very serious. We learned of the Pearl Harbor bombing on our way to Toronto. We were all dead serious and now I am feeling sorry for myself because Charles asked me to marry him and I refused him."

"Refused him? Why? I thought you loved him"

"I do. What was I thinking? Forget it. I don't want to talk."

I had refused Charles's proposal, but regretted the whole scene. I regretted that he'd proposed to me. I wasn't ready. I never regretted being with him and I was always ready to see him, feel his arms around me, have him near me, touch me. A gentleman and a scholar, he was kind and adventurous in love and life. That was Charles. What more could I ask?

Charles took the war in stride and lived life as fully as he could, as did the rest of Great Britain.

The English newspapers carried more hometown news than news from the fronts. Ethel enjoyed reading local stuff and talking about what she'd read. But, for goodness sakes, who in their right mind would want to get married and maybe bring a baby into this world at this time? Not me that was for sure, that would only be another nightmare.

"Hmm, so the girl down the street, she delivered the baby at home with a midwife nun. No hospital space for maternity cases. I heard she did great. The baby is a healthy boy."

"Midwife, really?" I barely understood the meaning of the word and I didn't want to voice what I was thinking. I couldn't. The emotional rollercoaster from the heights of love and lust with Charles to the pits of bewilderment piled atop the trauma of my job overwhelmed me. I rubbed my arms, thinking of what to say to Ethel so as not to upset her with my miserable mood.

"Do you mind cleaning up, Ethel? I'm not

thinking straight. I really need to lie down and rest."

"No, I don't mind, sweetie. You go on."

"Hope no sirens tonight." I touched my forehead and made the Sign of the Cross on the bump. "I work the night shift tomorrow so I'll sleep in."

"Right, good night, I'll be really quiet," Ethel said and busied herself in the kitchen.

"Night."

The next day I awoke around noon in a much better mood. Ethel was at work so I had the apartment to myself. I dressed in my white blouse and long brown skirt. I put on my green army sweater and walked out of the dark apartment house hallway into bright sunlight.

Some neighbors were sitting on their front steps enjoying the warm July day. I stopped to chat.

"Good day, Mrs. Jackson," I said to a woman who lived a few doors away. "How are you today?"

"Oh, just dandy, love. Oh my, and what happened to you?" she said, looking up from her knitting with a sunny smile and a missing tooth.

"Just bumped into the door in the dark." I fed her the white lies as all good secret agents did. What was that? A venial sin? I wouldn't have to confess that, but what about the entire book of rules? All the rule breaking I committed with Charles. Oh my God. What would I say in confession? I knew at once that I would never see the dark inside of a confessional again.

"Say, do you know where I could buy a little

jumper like that for a baby?" I had decided then and there to celebrate the new baby down the street with a gift. After all, he was the hope of the future as Ethel had said.

"Sure, Come inside. I have one or two you may like," Mrs. Jackson said and led me into her cozy flat.

"Lived here since the end of the last war," she said as I looked around at her mementos and photos on the mantel.

"Who is this handsome one?" I asked picking up a framed photo of a young man in military uniform, but not a uniform from this day and age.

"...at's my mate, Harry S. Jackson. Such a handsome chap, he was. Lived through that last war and passed on just about two years ago. A fine fellow he was. He took care of me and our son just fine. Never missed a day of work in his life. You know, missy, I still love that man."

"Oh, I'm so sorry for your loss. I didn't mean to bring up sad feelings and—"

"No bother. I like talking about him. Keeps him alive in my heart, you know. This is my son. His name is Robert. Robert Harold Jackson. Don't he look just like his ol' man? Acts like him too. Patriotic and all. Chews his food the same way, too. Ain't that a laugh?"

"I see he is a fly-boy. Right? Royal Air Force. You must be very proud of him?" I said.

"T'at's the truth. Now, come in here with me and see what you like."

Mrs. Jackson brought me into her bedroom and opened a storage trunk at the foot of the bed. It overflowed with baby sweaters, booties and blankets. "I sit here every night after dinner and knit as fast as I can. It occupies my mind and keeps my hands busy. You know what they say, about idle hands being the devil's work?"

"Yes, I do remember that."

"I have to take these to the convent tomorrow. The nun midwives bring them to the new babies. Might you like to help me bring them there?

"Sure, I could do that in the afternoon. They're very beautiful, Mrs. Jackson."

"Well, take what you like. Is it for the new boy down the street?" she asked.

"Yes." I was feeling so good. I was actually smiling again and felt connected to the world.

"Well, he already has one just like this." She held up a tiny jumper the size of her two hands. "Take this other one. It's a bit different. See it has a collar for the cooler weather and is a mite bigger for when he grows some. I am sure Elizabeth, his grandmother, will love it. So will his mom. She is a wonderful girl. You could be friends with her. Maybe help out with the baby when you're not working. Would you like that? Take you mind off things. You'd like her."

"Oh, I love this little jumper, too." I held up another from the trunk. "I'll take both to her. Thank you. How much do I owe you, Mrs. Jackson?"

"Never mind that. Just keep that for yourself. You dun have to pay me. The Red Cross gives me the yarn. And call me Molly, please. My name is Molly Jackson."

"Thank you, Molly. These are just perfect. I'll

see you tomorrow about this time. Oh, and my name is Marie Gentile. Just call me Marie. I live at number 421 on the first floor."

She wrapped the sweaters in some brown paper and walked me to the door. We confirmed our plan to meet and I had another idea.

"Do you think I could have some yarn, too. I love to knit and I could make socks for the troops."

"Sure, sweetheart. I'll get it ready for tomorrow."

"Thanks again, Molly. See you tomorrow."

Oh thank you God. I just made a friend outside work and I feel wonderful. I liked Molly. I could identify with her. She was a widow with her only son flying dangerous bombing missions with the RAF. She spent her days knitting socks and sweaters for the troops. In the evenings she worked feverishly on baby clothes. Most of all she was alive and living life as it was.

I could be like her. I'm a widow. I work feverishly…coding and decoding messages to and from the occupied countries keeping our soldiers safe and the resistance movements alive. I could be happy like Molly if I just let myself.

I resolved then and there that I would be happy and grateful for what I had and not worry about what was missing or what I might lose. I knew I would marry Charles Stanhope someday. That would be if he still wanted me after all the fuss I'd been making.

Chapter Eighteen

June, 1944

MAPS OF FRANCE, SWITZERLAND, AND Germany littered the kitchen table in front of our dinner dishes. I was headed for Munich and had to learn the escape routes should I need them. Adrenaline pumped through my veins putting me on edge.

Marie and I ate what we could of our dinner. The danger of my impending mission hung in the room. What if I were found out? How safe were the safe houses? Did I have the right identification papers? What if I were hauled off to a concentration camp? One unintended action or word would create havoc for me.

"Such a beautiful sunset," Marie said as the last rays came through the kitchen window at the townhouse.

"It will be dark in a few minutes. I have to leave for the pier in an hour," I whispered. We always whispered at the townhouse when it came to talking about our work for fear of someone listening.

Marie finished the last of her dinner then stood to clear the table. I drank my precious tea and smiled behind my cup as I admired the movement of her hips and the long line of her legs down to her thick socks. That was Marie. Sexy even in thick socks.

I loved all of her and thought what if I never saw her again? Would she know that I loved her? Would she understand how much I loved her? I never could find the right words to convince her. Would she ever marry me?

"Come here, darling," I said. Would I come back to her? Would I live through this mission?

She came, sat on my lap and leaned over the table to look at the maps.

I reached around her waist and nuzzled the sweet spot under her ear.

"Hmmm, very romantic," she said as she wiggled her bottom on my thighs. She kissed my forehead.

"You know the code to use when you call me," she whispered and tickled my ear with her sweet breath.

"Yes, darling." I nibbled her shoulder.

"Whom are you going to meet and where?" She continued our usual review before a mission.

"Karl Fleischer in Munich," I said with my lips close to her mouth.

"And why?" she said.

"To see for myself how Karl Fleischer eliminated the student resistance movement at the university," I answered and kissed her other shoulder.

"Hmm. I can't believe his name. Did you know Fleischer actually means butcher in German?" she said with her arms tightening around her own waist and torso shivering.

"Well, that is what he is. Butchering students in the name of protecting the Third Reich," I said, moving my eyes over the map of Germany she held up.

"Yes," she said. "Don't get distracted. Stay focused." Then she reviewed my contacts again.

In between kissing her, I said, "He is going to teach me the protocol so that we can implement it here after they occupy England."

"Yes, I am sure he will be happy to do that, too." She put the map on the table and reached for my eyeglasses, placing them on top of the map. She ran her fingers through my hair. She leaned into me and I kissed her luscious lips.

After a few minutes, I said, "Darling, I have to go save what is left of the world." I sat her on the table and prepared to leave, rolling my shirtsleeves down and taking my jacket from the back of my chair.

Smoke from the coal furnaces of London and mist from the river settled over the streets as I walked to a secluded abandoned wharf near the mouth of the Thames. I lit a cigarette, the signal to alert the captain of the German U-boat to surface. I had to wait another twenty minutes before the sub came into view.

"Herr Stanhope?" a female voice with a German accent asked. I could feel her behind me.

"No. Herr Gerber. You?" I asked for the German handler's code name.

"Frauline Either. Shall we go?"

I turned to face her. She gave me a toothy grin and then led me toward the end of the wharf where the U-boat hid in the dark murky waters of the high tide.

"Before you step onto the boat a hatch will open in front of you. Turn to face me and carefully step down backwards onto the ladder. Be careful the interior will be dark so trust your instincts. When you reach the bottom, just stand still. Someone will pass by you and ascend the ladder and close the hatch. After that, low lights will illuminate the interior, the boat will leave the wharf for deeper water, and the captain will greet you thereafter."

The German captain, proud of his boat and his knowledge, gave me a guided tour from stem to stern. It was a small boat by submarine standards, but capable of moving fast and striking with deadly torpedoes.

"This here is the newest model. Some 588 such boats are submerged around the English Isles, Norway, and Sweden and in the Bay of Biscayne. We will win this war with these little ships. We will take England and Spain as well as the United States."

"Yes, I see how that will work." I said. "I understand there are many along the Florida coastline. Is that right?"

"Yah, there are."

The devastation of our naval forces flashed before my eyes. Fires on the shores of Florida burned into my imagination. Would this damn war ever end in victory for the Allies? I shook my head to clear away deadly pictures.

"And here, sir, are the best torpedoes in the world. I do not believe that even the Japanese have these," he said with an arrogant smile.

"Hmmm, very good. Very nice indeed," I said. My mouth went dry. I believed what I heard and the importance of my mission, not only to find out the protocol for uncovering the resistant students, but also to find out every piece of information I could. I had to get this information about the new U-boat and torpedoes back to the Major as soon as possible. It could not wait for my return from Munich. The Allies would benefit more now than in three weeks when I was due to return to England.

"There is no doubt. This will be the most successful submarine attack in navel history," he repeated. "The German Type VII U-boat is a wonderful machine. It is covert and agile. Simply wonderful. Ah…" He paused and then said, "The German mind for engineering is marvelous. Do you not agree?"

"Yes, certainly, it is magnificent. Powerful too," I said as my heart fell into my stomach. This could be the turning point of the war in favor of Hitler if it were successful.

"Absolutely, Herr Gerber. We will win this war. I promise you, Spain and England will be occupied by Germans very shortly," the captain said as he escorted me to a small compartment with a bed. You may rest here and I will come for you when we arrive at the Hamburg wharf. He threw his head back, puffed out his chest and raised his arm in the Nazi salute. His righteousness apparent in his posture. "Heil, Hitler," he shouted.

"Heil Hitler," I said with a rock in my throat, clicked my heels and returned the salute before closing the compartment door.

I disembarked at Hamburg with a sour taste.

My transport was a Zundapp KS750s motorcycle with a sidecar driven by a boy of about thirteen. Wearing a Nazi uniform a size too big for his lean frame, his enthusiasm for the Reich was evident. He saluted with a snappy hand and then drove like a wild man through the streets of Hamburg to the train station. Luckily, no pedestrians crossed our path. Nevertheless, a poor scrawny cat sat at the side of the road and the boy driver aimed straight at it. He ran over the cat and laughed. Lucky the sidecar opened to the fresh air. I spit up as he picked up speed. God help us if we did not win this war. This boy and others like him would be our future leaders. I vomited on the side of the road when he let me off next to the train station.

As I waited to board my train, soldiers with rifles guarded the platform. They marched up and down in pairs checking identification papers. I heard the sound of steel breaks on the tracks and smelled the steam vapor from another train that pulled into the station. The faces of young soldiers first peered out the windows and then descended onto the platform waiting for orders. Some were tight-lipped while other jostled each other like children. They smelled of sweat and dirt. Some wore bloody bandages on their hands or feet. One walked by me on crutches. I looked down at his hurt foot. It was black with frostbite.

Nevertheless, the crowd offered me an opportunity to duck unnoticed into a private room where there was a phone for public use. Marie took the call and we spoke in Italian. The whole conversation was in the code we had prepared. I alerted her to the U-boats and she would tell the Major straight away. I completed the call quickly to avoid suspicion.

"Everyone get up and go to the platform." Some soldiers boarded my train just as I reached my compartment. Moving from car to car they barked orders for everyone to get off. "Civilians off. Come on, move, you fools, take your bags. This train no longer will go to Munich. Wait for the next one."

"But, my daughter is waiting for me." An old woman cried and wiped her rummy eyes with her stained handkerchief.

"Lady, what is it? Do you not understand German? Take the next train," a soldier shouted closer to her ear. "You toothless old witch," said his brute of a partner as he pushed the butt of his rifle into her shoulder. The woman cried out in pain and despair.

I saw firsthand that one didn't have to be a Jew to be treated like someone less than human. My heart went out to her. What if that woman had been my mother? But as Herr Gerber, I could not help her more than carry her bag. Any other actions might have revealed me as either a traitor to Germany or a madman. Both would have caused suspicion.

The Munich train station was deserted. Only the old lady and I had stepped off the train and she disappeared around the corner of the building. Two men closed in behind me. Something poked my ribs.

"Herr Stanhope?" How did they know? What had I done to tip anyone off? Or was there a mole in our organization? I did not have time to think about it. I had to escape right now when my chances were the best.

"Nein, Gerber. Herr Gerber…from Hamburg. My papers?" I said in German and reached inside my raincoat. It was now or never. I had to run. Chances of capture later were far greater than right now. Instead of papers I pulled out my pack of Turkish cigarettes. Soldiers always appreciated cigarettes.

One grabbed the entire pack. The other held his gun pointed at my chest.

"Danka (thanks)." They laughed, tore the papers, and one put the pieces in his breast pocket.

I took out my gold lighter and they grabbed it to light their cigarettes. Their second drag sent both men face down onto the concrete platform smashing the faces, crushing their noses and bleeding from their mouths. For a split second I looked down and regretted what I had done to those two young men with the poisoned cigarettes from MI6. Then I ran like hell to jump on the last train going south toward Switzerland. I had to get out of Germany fast. My capture would mean instant execution. The Swiss border was my best bet, but I had to make it there first.

I lay on the settee in the major's office. We blew smoke rings. He made them with his cigar and I, with my Turkish cigarettes.

"The gold lighter did the trick, sir, along with every soldier's yen for cigarettes. The train trip was quite uneventful. I managed to avoid the inspectors every time. It was the aerial tram that did me in. It started to move across the chasm to Switzerland just before I reached the platform and I had to jump for it and through the window."

We both laughed and I winced at the pain from my taped rib cage. "It was not that funny, sir." Then I laughed again. "Ouch."

Marie had laughed the night before when I begged her, "No lovemaking tonight, darling."

CHAPTER NINETEEN

I SAT AS THE CENTER of attention at the meeting of the German sympathizers outside London. Their mood was fouled by the news I, their most trusted informer, delivered. As an MI6 agent for Great Britain I usually misinformed this group so they could not damage the cause to defeat Hitler. They passed bogus info to their counterparts in the occupied countries. I had been successful with the false information and the Germans had bombed dummy tanks during the Allies' push towards Berlin.

"At this point in time, gentlemen, I am sorry to inform you that the thousand year plan of the Reich is literally going up in flames as we speak," I said with glee in my heart but worry enacted on my brow, furrowing with lines of discontent. "Allied bombs burned Hamburg. More than thirty thousand people died there, as well as more in Dresden and in other German cities now burning to the ground. Sadly many innocents have had to die." They did not understand my emotion.

"What about the other countries, Charles? Is there no hope for the Reich to live on in at least one? What about the Netherlands? Or Norway? We were so strong there."

"Well, sir, if I may say so. The Luftwaffe's strategy has been aimless. Their intelligence gathering has been faulty. Communication and supply lines were restored with vigor. Italy has surrendered; Mussolini was captured and will probably be hanged. Our dear Führer is in hiding with his beloved, Eva, and his most trusted associates. I understand his heart fails and he suffers signs of Parkinson and has attempted suicide. Only time will tell his ultimate fate."

"So, then we have altogether lost?" said another man with an incredulously soured voice. "Do you think ruin faces Germany for now?"

"I find it difficult to believe the Reich will rise again in our lifetimes. Not to the status it has been. It simply does not have the capacity even with your support... General Zhukov has the Russian troops ready to take Berlin any day. Sorry to say it will be an easy task. I understand the German troops in Berlin are out of ammunition. What do you think that indicates, sir? To be blunt, I fully expect Hitler will surrender within a few days, maybe even hours."

"How soon did you say? It is implausible that Hitler is leaving his soldiers without bullets. Do we have time to send ammunition?"

"Well, sir, that is a splendid idea, but how would we get it to them? After all, the Americans are on the ground in France, Italy, and Germany where the Führer's troops are now surrendering."

A door slammed. The room suddenly flooded with uniformed coppers wielding nightsticks. Men shouted and chaos broke out as everyone shot out of their seats in outrage. I slipped out the French door onto the patio and waited just outside to listen as the self-righteous Nazi sympathizers headed for jail and trial as traitors.

I heard the constable say, "Gentlemen, please remain calm. Stay seated. Do not bother to resist. My boys are crawling over the grounds surrounding the entire estate. My orders are to inform you that you are all under arrest."

Lord Sommers shouted, "Humph, arrest? What for? Why, I am simply having a drink with my friends. This is entirely preposterous. We are a card-playing club, here. You cannot arrest us."

Members of the police brigade handcuffed each and everyone. The men shot out of their seats again. One made a run for the door to no avail. Commotion filled the room as the wives came in from the parlor. The ladies were crying. One screamed her husband's name. The men were still in utter disbelief.

"For treason, my lord."

"Treason? How dare you say that word me, a member of the House of Lords."

"Better to say giving aid and comfort to the enemy, stealing monies from your tenants to send to Mussolini, using your positions of power to jeopardize the safety of our countrymen both here and abroad. Is that more precise for you, sir?"

"What in the world? Pardon me, before we go any further. You cannot just come marching in here with guns and handcuffs, and…and…"

"Oh, begging your pardon sir, but we can. We have our orders," said the chief.

"Preposterous, show me your documents. Evidence, do you have evidence?" one of the Nazi sympathizers hollered.

"Well now, sir, I am not privy to that information. You will learn more at the precinct, I suppose. Now, move along quietly, sirs, and we can get you where you have to go. You will talk to those with more authority and knowledge than I, sir."

The coppers took the men by the arms and lined them up in front of the fireplace. The men were angry rather than fearful and continued to protest.

"What, what, what does this mean for us, Charles? Charles, where are you?" Sommers looked over his shoulder at the open patio door. "Charles, where the hell are you?" he whispered, "You bastard. You two-timer low-down scum traitor of a Nazi, show yourself."

"Well of all the…" grumbled the older gentleman with a gravy stain on his shirt as he followed the others to the paddy wagon waiting in the drive. Oaths of denial persisted. Astonished as they were going out the door, they thought their conspiring and sympathies for the Nazis were negotiable.

"Charles Stanhope, show your face, you coward!" another shouted.

I smiled, lit a cigarette, walked to the Aston Martin and drove away without regret. As I checked the rearview mirror, I saw the house windows lit from within every room as the coppers gathered evidence.

Charles came to my flat that night. He dropped his long torso onto the sofa, stretched out long legs and kicked off his shoes. He took out one of his all time favorite smokes, relaxing now after the exhaustion of the past strenuous months. I kissed him lightly on the lips before taking a cigarette for myself then paced while waiting for him to speak.

"So?"

"What?" His head was back and his eyes closed.

"So what happened?" The suspense unnerved me. He didn't say anything. "Charles, darling, for goodness sakes, what happened tonight?" I was exasperated to no end with this man. I could never anticipate his actions or reactions.

"Oh, nothing much. They will probably all hang for treason, I daresay." He put out his cigarette. "Russia will take Berlin in the next few days. Hitler will surrender or be murdered. The total surrender of the Germans will come soon after that."

He stood and brought me closer to him with his arm around my waist. He began to hum in my ear and started to sway.

"Well, Mr. Stanhope. Let's not think about that now. I have a bottle of wine the Major gave me. Let's celebrate your victory with the arrests." His heat melted me into his arms. I looked up into his blue eyes and reached for his lips.

"I have hero worship, you know," I said.

"And is the Major your hero, Miss Captain America?" He nuzzled the side of my neck.

"No, my hero is Charles Courageous Stanhope."

"Really? I like the sound of that. What can your hero do for you tonight?" He rubbed his hand over my back.

"Well, let's see…" I unbuttoned his shirt.

"Where is Ethel, love?" He was ever cautious and tentative with others around.

"She is at your townhouse with MacPherson," I said and opened his belt buckle.

"In one of those big beds and we have the single? Lucky Ethel. Lucky us. Hmm."

I took off his glasses. His mouth tasted like wine and honey where I lingered more than a moment and enjoyed his touch under my blouse on my bare back.

"I think we should stay right here, no hotel." I pushed him back onto the sofa. "I don't need much room."

Charles just moaned as he played with my hair. I won't repeat what he said, but it was all good.

That was April 30, 1945.

Ethel met me at the office the next morning.

Something was different. She had not tied back her hair in its usual victory roll, but had left it loose, tossed it to one side and her eyes shone. She smiled brightly.

"Hmm, somebody is happy today," I said and pulled her into the closet for privacy. "Tell me what happened."

"MacPherson proposed. Look." She held her hand

out and I saw a beautiful antique platinum ring with a stunning diamond.

"Oh, my God. Congratulations. I guess you said 'yes.'" We hugged like sisters and jumped with excitement. "When is the wedding?"

"As soon as Hitler surrenders." Ethel said.

"That could be today. Are you ready?"

"I am ready. You know I've been waiting for him to ask for months. He was so adorable. When he asked me, he went down on his knees and all. He acted shy."

"I'm so happy for you two." My day had come and gone. Charles had not mentioned marriage again. Who in the world would keep asking someone who had rejected him many times? I wouldn't blame him if he never asked again. Would I have to ask him?

In the office, the Teletype machine tapped out a message. Our two office mates had worked the night shift, so they were not there. I ran to get the message.

"Oh, my God, oh, my God," I said. "Ethel, hurry. Read this. I want to make sure it says what I think it says."

Ethel read the message. We looked at each other and let out screams to end all screams. The room next door erupted when they heard us. Ethel and I rushed out into the hallway to tell them. Then we ran upstairs to the major's office taking the steps two at a time with other staff who had heard us.

We burst through the door. I saw Charles in the

old leather chair in front of the major's desk. I heard him say, "In only a matter of hours…"

"Ladies?" the major asked. He dashed his cigar in the overflowing ashtray on the corner of the desk and we took deep breaths and composed ourselves.

I handed him the message without saying a word. He read it and handed it to Charles. He remained calm and collected.

"Call the rest of the team, please, from every floor in this building. Bring them all here." He stared at us and we stared back.

"Quick, hop to it!" We stared at him for a moment then hurried throughout the building banging on doors, walls, and railings.

"Quick, come to the Major's office, quick," we shouted.

When everyone gathered, the Major read aloud.

"May 1, 1945, Red Army took Berlin. Found bunker empty except for the Goebbels and their six children dead. Evidence of cyanide found, Hitler and Eva's bodies believed burned, few bones. Only jaw and skull recovered in garden pit." Tears streamed down the major's face.

The staff looked at each other in stunned relief, and then cheered.

"Hooray!" Hugs and kisses went around the room and the major passed a bottle of Bourbon.

Charles held me tight with one arm around my waist and the other around my shoulder. I closed my eyes and felt his warm lips on my cheeks right there in front of everyone, "Now, will you marry me, Marie Gentile?"

I looked into his gorgeous blue eyes. Why had I

ever thought I wouldn't marry this handsome courageous sexy man? Oh for goodness sakes, why the heck did I doubt him or myself?

"Yes, Charles Stanhope, I've loved you since the first day I saw you. You, my dear man, are my hero, my superman, my Captain Britannia, my secret agent, my one, and only, my man.

"I love you, too," he said and placed a garnet ring on my left hand. "I have had this in my pocket for days. It was my mother's. Ian saved it and gave it to me for you."

"Oh, that is so sweet." I put my arms around his neck and kissed him.

He pulled away and turned to the group. With his arm still around my waist he announced, "Ladies, gentleman, I present the future, Mrs. Stanhope."

Whoops and cheers went up and we all took another drink of Bourbon and congratulated each other.

Then I fell into Charles's arms by way of missing the floor this time.

CHAPTER TWENTY

I OPENED MY EYES TO see another eye through the tiny hole in the center of the mirrored light on the doctor's forehead. I lay in the major's office on the yellow settee. I saw my reflection in the mirror and felt Charles's hand around mine.

"I fainted again, didn't I? I faint at the oddest moments, doctor. What's happening to me?" I asked with a troubled laugh. "I don't understand. This never happened before I…er…met Charles."

He leaned closer to me and whispered. "Might you be pregnant, my dear? Have any other symptoms?"

"No other symptoms, sir. I'm sure I am not pregnant."

"Happy to say, nothing serious then. Just a bit too much excitement and stress, and maybe not enough to eat, I suspect. God knows we were all under a great deal of stress before the exciting news of today."

"Anything I should do?"

"My prescription is stay away from alcoholic drinks, not even beer or wine. Make sure you eat throughout the day and you establish a regular sleep pattern. That should be easier now."

Charles said, "That is certainly wonderful news. Thank you, doctor."

"I'm feeling a lot better."

"Charles, get her something to eat soon. I presume there will not be any more sirens. The world is looking better. I want you to take this for a few months." He reached into his black bag and drew out a bottle of black thick syrup.

"Oh, for goodness sakes, what the heck is that? I said with disgust. "Looks like something I had to take as a child," I protested making an ugly face.

"Marie, just a tonic of vitamins from across the pond. It is probably the same one you used. One tablespoon daily will help you regain your stamina which you will need for your new married life." He winked at me with a fatherly grin.

"I will take this. I will need lots of stamina." Then I whispered to him, but I knew Charles heard me, "He is quite a man, you know."

Charles open the major's door and let everyone back in. They cheered again passed the bottle of bourbon. Everyone had another sip while I, the good patient, took a swig of my vitamin syrup.

"We should have a double wedding. What do you think?" Ethel asked.

"Yes, we have been through the war together, let's begin the peace together." I said, "What do you think, Charles?"

"Perfect," he said, "I am sure Mac will agree.

We'll ask him right away. I believe he is at the townhouse. Why not go there now?" Charles said.

I squeezed his arm in agreement.

"Of course." Ethel answered. "You two are so right. But I have to go to the flat to change."

My friend, Molly, was sitting outside her building knitting as usual. "Molly, meet this wonderful man. He has asked me to marry him for the third time. Do you think he means it?"

"I should say so. And you? What did you say this time, after the war maybe?"

In my excitement I forgot the English citizens had not yet heard the news. I looked at Charles and he nodded.

"Molly, the end of the war is very, very near. We heard today the Russians are in Berlin and Hitler is dead."

"What, what did you say?" Molly asked with tears already streaming.

"Hitler is dead and the Russians have taken Berlin," I repeated.

"Oh, my, Hitler is dead? Is that what you said? Oh, two good pieces of news." Her words belied her tearful emotions. Her small hands dropped the needles and yarn into her lap. Her blue eyes brimmed and her arms reached out to me.

I bent down to exchange hugs and kisses over and over.

"Thank God. Thank God," she prayed. She

recovered her composure and called into the
hallway. "Gwen, Mildred, come hear the news."
She turned and called to us. "When is the wedding?
I will make your wedding gown."

We celebrated at night, but we anguished during
the day. We were privy to news from the continent
describing the horrors in the work camps where the
Jews had been confined, starved and gassed.

We read messages from GI's who had found the
infirm, elderly and mentally ill chained to beds. The
machine ticked on with news from the Asia front.
Japan finally surrendered in August after massive
destruction by the atom bomb.

In the midst of all of this, life continued.
Children played in the streets, babies were born, and
the lights remained on all night. Charles and I
moved into his townhouse. MacPherson and Ethel
took over the flat. Charles convinced the Major to
close the office on some Mondays so we could have
long weekends.

"Love?" Charles said one Sunday morning.
"Shall we go for a whirl in the countryside? It is a
lovely day. Sunshine and all."

"Sure, why not? I'll be up in a minute." I
moaned from under the bedcovers.

"Martin will be so happy you remember how to
drive." He had been up. I smelled breakfast and
turned over to look at him.

"What? You cooked breakfast and you're going to
let me drive? Who are you? Where is Charles?"

"Come, it's getting late." He playfully pulled the covers off my naked body.

"Okay, okay."

It was the end of July and we enjoyed sunny days and short nights. I was hard-pressed to keep warm in the English summer without getting dressed quickly, so I jumped off the bed.

I dressed in a new camel wool tweed suit with slacks that I had bought at Harrods. It went perfectly with a green sweater Charles had given me. I put on some lipstick and headed downstairs for breakfast. Charles had already finished his and mine waited on top of the stove. He headed out the door as soon as I put my fork down. I didn't even have time to brush my hair properly.

I climbed into the driver's seat and drove the Aston Martin. Charles gave instructions on driving the machine and directions to the open road.

"You haven't told me where we're going, Charles. Do we have a destination? I know this is not the way to Liverpool which is the only other city I have seen in England."

"We are heading west. I want to show you something. Turn right at the next intersection just ahead. Then make the next left. Slow down, love. It comes quickly."

After we made the left I said, "What could possibly be on this dusty dirt road, darling? Tell me. No, never mind. I love surprises."

"There on the right. Stop there at that green gate."

I did and looked beyond it to a path with trees

lining both sides and summer wild flowers of all
colors growing in the meadow beyond.

"Oh, Charles, what a lovely place. How did you
ever find it?"

"Come, let's go in."

"Charles, no. Doesn't anyone live here?"

"Not yet. We will soon. My brothers have agreed
that it should be ours."

"Ours? Oh, for goodness sakes, Charles, why
didn't you tell me?"

"I know how you love surprises. I do want to
show you the cottage."

"A cottage, too."

We walked along the curved path, which passed
a pond. A white duck and four browns ones feasted
on the underwater buffet. A gray owl hidden behind
deep green oak leaves kept watch. As we made our
way around the last curve, I stopped short at the
sight of a thatch roof.

"Oh, my God. Is that what Englishmen call a
cottage? It is beautiful and…big…big enough for a
large family. I'm speechless. Can we go inside?" I
asked. My voice choked with tears. I loved this
man. He always overwhelmed me.

One quiet evening after a dinner of Charles's
famous mutton stew, we sat in the living room
with the French door open to the garden. It was the
end of August and the sun headed for its sleepy
autumn in England. Molly had encouraged me to
knit and that evening I worked on a child's blanket

for the orphanage. Charles read the *Daily Mail*.

"Love, we haven't set a wedding date. Tomorrow shall we go for our documents and then visit the parsonage for a day and time?"

"I think we should wait…"

"What? No, not again. You, darling, are very exasperating." He stood hovering over me. His hand covered my cheek with a tender touch and I kissed his palm. "Now, tell me again, why wait?

"Just until the city settles down and we can celebrate our personal victory aside from the peace and I want to wait for Mario and Angie. They are my only family, you know and what about your brothers and sister?"

"The boys still have to get a lift back from Germany and France."

"So, then let's wait a few more weeks. I want our families with us. What about your sister?"

"My sister? We haven't heard from her in two months."

"Oh, Charles, I am so sorry. Why didn't you tell me?" I thought of her falling in love with a romantic Frenchman and living her life, maybe in Nice with a clear blue sky and no fog ever.

"I thought you would faint."

"Stop that talk, I am not fainting any more. I feel fine.

"She is not missing, love. She worked with a partisan cell," he said. The he mumbled, "In Italy, so I think she is quite safe."

"Where did you say? I didn't hear you."

He looked down. His beautiful blue eyes avoided looking at me. He swept his hand through his hair.

Then he took off his glasses and cleaned them with his shirttail.

"Italy, love,"

"You said, Italy. Am I right?

"Yes, love, Italy. She has been there a few years." He said in cautious monotone. He lit a cigarette and inhaled deeply.

"A few years? Do you mean two or three years, Charles? I crossed my arms over my heaving chest. My breath came short and fast.

"Yes, a few."

"Oh, my God. Why are you pacing? What the hell did you do?" I poked his chest with my knitting needle. "Damn it. You gave her my job, didn't you?" I exploded, "Italy? Italy?"

I poked him again. He grabbed my wrists.

"Didn't you? Didn't you, Mr. Stanhope? You are a nefarious sneaky controlling man, Charles Stanhope. You lied to me," I said in a loud whisper like a bluster of winter wind.

My Italian temper took over. My blood boiled. I swallowed hard, walked into the house and slammed the door. My head ached and my heart was broken.

Had my Charles Stanhope lied to me? I couldn't even remember what he said about my staying in London. It was so long ago. Suddenly exhaustion crept like a welcome stranger into my bones. I just wanted to sleep. I looked around the bedroom room and imagined myself back in my apartment in New Jersey. Living alone again seemed so simple. Betrayed, alone and in a foreign country with a man I thought I knew. Oh, God, come help me.

Charles was next to me with his arm across my pillow when I awoke. I turned on my side and faced him, pulling the covers up to my neck. I was not ready to bare even my outer self to him.

"It wasn't what you think. Can you listen now, darling without a temper tantrum?"

"I'll try." I coughed and cleared my throat.

"I did not want to hurt you or disappoint you. The decision was not only about you and me, love."

"Did your sister want to go more than I did?" I said. "Is that why I'm here and she's there?"

He didn't answer. Instead he fished for a cigarette on the nightstand and lit up.

I had a chance to think. What if Charles had not encouraged the change in my orders? *What if I had gone to Italy?* I was fooling myself thinking I had wanted to go. I loved Charles. He was the par excellence, primo, peerless in my book. I would not have traded him for Italy. Oh, for goodness sakes, what was I thinking? I had everything wanted.

"War is complicated, Marie. You know that. My sister was already in France. It was easy to slip across the border to Italy. Besides she had traveled the continent many times and you had never. She knew Italy inside and out. She had studied in Italy and Germany. She was the best candidate. I am sorry, Marie. You would have stood out as an American to the Germans who have a very good knowledge of the Italians. More than language skills mattered. Besides, I could not bear to put you in that danger."

"Oh?"

"Only God knows what the Nazis would have done to you if you were found out by some little mistake like holding a cigarette like an American. I held back my sister's role from you then because of secrecy. I had to protect her as much as you."

"Yes. I'm sorry. I'm so egocentric at times. Still love me?" I snuggled close to him. His body still tantalized me as it did the first time I saw him. "Remember the morning we met at the diner?

"Yes, I distinctly remember you trying to get me to stay in Farview that night."

"You do? Was I that transparent or are you just perceptive?"

"Perceptive, love." He chuckled, put out his cigarette and tickled my ribs, kissing my mouth ever so sweetly.

"It was love at first sight, Marie," he whispered as he nuzzled my neck with his lips. He caressed my shoulders. "Hmm…and you were so insistent I sit at the counter. Who could resist you?"

"Don't know." I didn't speak as his smooth hands roamed over me. "Who could resist *you*?"

"Come closer, love. Yes, right there."

We married in September. Molly had insisted that the night before the wedding Charles had to stay at the townhouse and I with her.

"You should not see each other the night before the wedding. It's a tradition for brides and grooms."

She had become so dear to us that we would have done anything she asked.

Our wedding day was sunny and warm. Sunbeams streamed through windows. The minister had placed some wildflowers on the altar

I wore the beautiful new gown Molly and her friend, Gwen, had stitched from parachute silk. They had sewn delicate crocheted lace stars and pearls from a broken necklace around the sweetheart neckline and scattered throughout the bodice. My sister-in-law, Mario's wife, brought me a blue silk garter, new lingerie and stockings from the States. Ethel had bought a pair of white shoes. She lent them to me. Old, new, borrowed and blue.

I stood at the door of the chapel with my arm through Mario's. When I saw Charles waiting for me at the end of the aisle, I held my breath and remembered the first time his blue eyes had penetrated my defenses. His fine handsome face and blond hair still sent sizzles down the back of my legs. He was my man and I loved him.

Charles's brothers stood with him at the altar. His sister was not able to come. She had met her true love, not in a diner, but in a barn outside Anzio just before the Americans landed. I didn't think anyone in the far future would ever believe her or me about where we met our husbands.

ℰPILOGUE

Charles and I moved into the cottage. The house was large enough to have Molly live with us along with our two orphan girls, Catherine and Mary. They were just eight years old when we brought them home. Both girls had been evacuated from London to the same farm in Wales as babies during the Blitz. They grew up as sisters there and then in our home. They wanted to find their parents. Unfortunately we did locate them. They were listed as deceased on documents we found in the Bureau of War Records. They had perished in the wretched bombings of London.

Spy work remained an integral part of Charles's life as England fought the ensuing Cold War. He never did raise sheep as he had once dreamed. He left that to me and our daughters. He and his brothers continued with the secret service and later with the Mossad.

We opened our house to Jews liberated from the

concentration camps and helped them reunite with their families when possible.

In 1950 I traveled to New York City to meet my friend Ruth. It was the first time I had been back to the States since leaving on the troop ship. So much had happened since we planned the date back in training camp and she left for undercover work in Paris with Rick. We never located Rick.

An American infantryman had found Ruth hiding in a wine cellar. Later on she married him. They lived on a dairy farm in western New Jersey with their twins.

Ethel and MacPherson moved to the United States in 1946. MacPherson became a U.S. citizen and both he and Ethel worked for the CIA as undercover agents during the Cold War. They devoted their lives cleaning up the aftermath of the war and stopping the spread of communism from hungry Russia.

Mario and Angie move to Italy. They bought an old dilapidated piece of a barn and transformed it into a sweet bed and breakfast. We brought our daughters there for the twelve days of Christmas every year. Angie would teach them to cook Italian style and Mario would tell them stories about America, enticing them to go to Cornell University in upstate New York. I wished they would decide to stay with us in England, but the decision was theirs.

Coming 2015

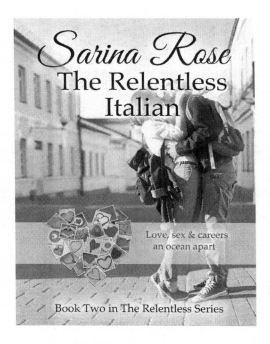

Sadie saw through the leaded glass side panel.
Tony Andriosi the heartthrob of St Joseph College
graduating class leaned against the porch column.
She hadn't seen Tony all day and missed his clear
blue eyes and the attention he paid her. She liked
him, but this was going too far. Following her to
Rosemary's house?

Coming 2015

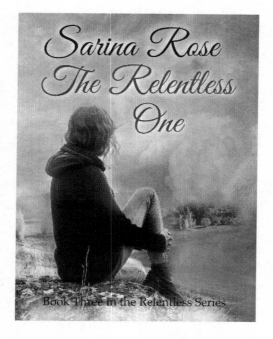

Conventional? Not on your life. Eve O'Hara's love bound her to Angelo. Their own decisions ruled and dictated their own actions. Eve and Angelo had their own recipe. They had the ingredients. Was it a recipe for happiness or disaster?

ABOUT THE AUTHOR

Sarina Rose was born to first generation Italian-American parents in New Jersey. She was influenced by her childhood growing up in the four-family apartment house built by their grandfather and his friends in the early 20th century. Her mother's family, living only about five miles away, were often sources of family history. Her father's family occupied the four apartments throughout her childhood into her late teens. The families took their meals together and she wandered through the apartments at will.

She is a member of Space Coast Authors of Romance and Romance Writers of America®. She quilts children's blankets for local hospitals and wheelchair bags for nursing homes, serves as docent at the Ruth Funk Center for Textile Arts at the Florida Institute of Technology and leads a lively discussion of publishing at S.A.I.L. (Senior Adventures in Learning).

To learn more, become a member of Sarina's street team, or receive her newsletter, send an email to *sarinarose@outlook.com.*

Made in the USA
Charleston, SC
19 October 2016